HAND TREMBLER

**Books
by
Gerald Hausman**

GUNS
Turtle Dream
Ghost Walk
Tunkashila

STAR SONG *series*
Evil Chasing Way
Hand Trembler

Coming Soon!
Sungazer
Book **3**

HAND TREMBLER

GERALD HAUSMAN

SPEAKING VOLUMES, LLC
NAPLES, FLORIDA
2018

Hand Trembler

ISBN 978-1-62815-838-0

For Kurt and Erica

"And then he went to the top of the mountain and dressed himself in woodpecker feathers, then he started down the mountain and changed to nuthatch, then he changed to small woodpecker, and at the foot of the mountain he changed to mountain tanager, then to flicker and when he came down to the prairie he put on sparrow feathers, then bluebird feathers and finally turned into *tseh-nul-tsosi*, rock wren."

Hasteen Klah, 1936

Chapter One

Doctor Frey died the other day.

That may not mean anything to some of you. At the end, he wasn't very well known. By the time I met the old scientist and abductee, he was already in eclipse, and quite bitter about it. He had liked being famous. He had liked signing the many editions of his books in so many foreign languages.

When I went down to Alamogordo to see him one last time, his wife, always protective, wouldn't open the door but an inch. I saw her sharp nose and teeth and heard her say, "Go away."

I explained who I was—granted more than ten years had passed between us, but she had very much liked the way I wrote about her husband, and as far as I knew, she liked me personally, but now the door closed and I was out in the hot desert wondering where to go.

Etienne had been deported years before and I had only heard from him once: "It wasn't an extraterrestrial that molested us in our sleeping bags. It was a bear." Molested was the wrong word. The creature had jerked us off. Bears don't do that. I told him in an email; he never wrote back. His Filipino healer with whom he worked had been jailed and deported, too. So that was the end of that.

Gomez was dead. Heart attack? Cancer? I don't remember which, but he'd become quite famous as a bounty hunter of outer-space aliens, and he'd written a book or two like all the rest of us.

My own book, or books, I wrote two of them, had made a little stir. One even made it to the screen. But I began to get death threats and for a long while I stopped writing altogether.

I still get strange hand-written letters, sometimes in ancient script, hand printed expressions of devotion for both books, defending the natives mostly and railing against the bad guy developers and the white supremacist secret police of America.

One devotee of the books phoned me every year for about twenty years. Another excoriated me for not continuing the series. She blasted me and begged me to keep on and I heard from her once every three years. My wife Laura said there was "a boxcar full of these odd people … not that many but at least one boxcar, and they all want something from you, another book, usually." She was right. One of them threatened me if I didn't deliver. "Send word or we'll take it from there," he said. The rest of his message was written in Hebrew and a native language I didn't know.

The worst of these boxcar people was a guy who blamed the death of his mother on me. He said she'd had the book spread-eagled on her chest when they found her stone-cold dead. He wrote me a twelve-page, single-spaced letter. He said he was coming to see me, and we'd "see about it then."

At the same time, a guy in a Georgia federal prison said he was also coming to see me "to set the record straight." He praised my novel, which he said he'd read in the prison library. He was on his way.

I asked my close friend, Roger Zelazny, what I should do about it. He said, "You can meet him in a restaurant of your choice, a crowded one preferably. You get there first and study the people as they come in. When this "fan" enters, you'll know instantly whether to sit down with him or not." Roger's advice was always golden.

I did what he said. The man came into Diego's in Santa Fe and I saw him, recognized him right away. There was something about him. I hadn't seen a photograph of the man but I knew he was the one as he stood there peering around looking for me.

I greeted him and we sat down, ordered coffee, and talked for about an hour or so. He was a very interesting man, if a bit bent, politically speaking.

Then he said he had to be on the road again. He thanked me for my time, said he would always cherish my book. I told him there were two. He said the one was enough. He read it like a Bible. As we left Diego's I asked him what he'd done to land in prison and he said, "I blew up a building."

Chapter Two

Some months ago, I got blown up myself.

Struck by lightning.

It wasn't a direct hit or I wouldn't be writing this.

But I am, and some part of me, most likely my lizard brain, believes it to be an accident.

Still, I don't believe in accidents. I believe in happenings.

When I got hit I was standing in our driveway, barefoot. I was also holding an umbrella and talking to some people in an SUV. It was raining very hard and the umbrella was a fool idea, or rather, no idea at all. I'd just grabbed it and headed out the door when I saw the black truck pull up in front of our gate.

There was a clap of thunder, a blind white flash.

Then my world turned the color of pink lemonade.

The "side strike" as it is often called, hit the truck first. That was the primary strike. It hit the truck, then the metal gate. Then me. I felt a peculiar surge run through my left hand which was resting on the hood of the truck.

It prickled weirdly up my left arm, danced across my chest, down my other arm, exiting out my right hand. In the process, I dropped my umbrella. It was all splayed and fried. A moment later, I discovered I was standing on it. Who knows how long. One thing I remember is talking to the people in the truck just as the lightning struck.

After that, my world shattered like an old acorn shell. I saw the people moving their lips, talking to me, but everything was soundless. I couldn't hear their voices or the rain clattering, or any engine noise.

I was deaf. The next little while the world went away.

***

Sometime later, I found myself in my favorite chair inside the house. Time had passed but I didn't know it. Our blue-fronted Amazonian parrot was laughing at me—I must've looked funny with my hair standing up—anyway, he was calling me an asshat.

I didn't know who I was, or for that matter, what I was. I was, but I didn't understand that either. I sat for a long time like that while Laura rubbed my shoulders and brought me glasses of water, some of which ran down the side of my mouth, as if my throat hadn't quite learned how to swallow yet.

Then my muscles started twitching. All down my back, mainly, but also there were small twitches, off and on, everywhere on my body. When the twitches felt more like pinches, I lay down on the cold tile floor. The quivery sensations ebbed away. For a couple more hours, I stayed flat out on the floor while the ghost of electricity played my bones like a xylophone. There was a music inside me and soon it put me to sleep.

When I woke, my mentor, Joogii, Bluejay DeGroat, was there, and he was talking softly to Laura and me. By this time I was stretched out on the couch, but I had no idea how I'd gotten there.

Jay was saying, "If you get hit by lightning, you're blessed. You're alive. But if you die, you go into the earth, with of course the blessing of the Earth Mother. Afterwards the ground all around where you got hit is considered sacred. That's the way we see it."

I had the presence of mind—now that I was coming back into myself—to ask him: "What happens now?"

Jay laughed, then grew serious again. He said, "You will carry the universe inside you. Stars, galaxies, black holes, all that's up there in the heavens, all of it just like a medicine bundle inside your body."

"What is lightning?" I asked.

"We call it zigzag. Snake deity."

"So I've been bitten but I live."

"You live," he said.

"One hell of a lucky strike," I told him.

"You'd been a tree, nobody'd go near you."

***

Time passed and I did, in some ways, live a different life.

And as Jay said, I thought of myself as a survivor, but more than that …
what about those galaxies in my gut? Were they still there? I can tell you this:
my sense of humor grew larger and my fear of death, that basic underlying
current of unconscious thought, it just wasn't there anymore.

My memory—for things long gone and lost in me—came back and I
could recite an endless list of primary school friends. Not only their names
but the streets where they lived and what their parents looked like. All this
from fifty years ago. Trapped in my brain and now floating free in memory.

Then there was my heart; it seemed to me it ran more smoothly now.

I felt it less. But more, in the spiritual sense.

One day after the strike I found myself crying over the story a homeless
man told me about how he was sitting in a bus heading to Santa Fe and the
girl sitting next to him who said she was a runaway told a policeman at the
bus station that he had kidnapped her.

The man was so woebegone and broken and luckless that when I stared
into his pale, lusterless, gin-colored eyes, I burst into tears, and he ended up
comforting me. I am still that way, comforting to some, and in need of comfort
myself. Lightning is a strange, and sometimes, munificent ally.

Chapter Three

I met a Cree Indian named Timbers Falling, who said he'd been struck by lightning four times. Each time, he said, he got wiser. His body weakened, then strengthened, and he somehow grew apart from people. But his heart was larger, spiritually speaking, he said. He loved people but he didn't have to be with them all the time.

"I was over in Vietnam," he told me, when the whole military operation came crashing down. This was at the very end, you understand. Saigon was coming down about our ears. People were running around like crazy. Military personnel were shipping out, flying out, running out of time to get out. I was one of the lucky ones. I packed my gear and went up into one of the tallest buildings where all the government guys hung out and guess what I found up on the sixth floor? The desks were just like normal, papers and file folders in place, lights on, everything normal. It was like five in the afternoon and I had to move fast if I wanted to get on a transport plane and fly back to base in the States.

"But there I was ass deep in the twilight zone. There were cigars still smoking in the ashtrays. Looking around, I saw a big stack of papers on a long grey metal desk. Guess what it was?"

I shrugged. "No idea."

"Military payment certificates. There was a big black market for these on the streets of Saigon. It was all monopoly money to me, so I stuffed this shit into my duffel and took the stairs down, down, down to the hot broil of the street, headed out to the tarmac and boarded a chopper. I got out of Saigon hours before the commies came in."

I had only one question.

"What'd you do with the bag?"

"Sent it to my mother back on the Rez."

"What did she do with it?"

"Stuck it under my bed. One year later I was discharged. I looked under the bed and there was my duffel where my mom had stowed it … Full of, what did I just call 'em? MPCs, military money. I cashed 'em and bought my mom a cute little house."

"Got any left?"

"All gone." He chuckled. "Hey, that was a fuck of a long time ago."

"So what do you do for a living now?"

"Housesit for people. When I'm not getting hit by lightning. What about you?"

"I write books. When I'm not getting hit by lightning."

He laughed.

I laughed.

We parted friends of the sky-fire night.

But it was no joking matter.

It was dead (so to say) serious.

I went back to the Navajo chants. They told the whole story of lightning. Not to mention the Diné birth into this, the fourth world. Let there be light was, as well, let there be lightning.

It was Elder Brother who gets struck first. Younger Brother rescues him, and the whole cycle and saga of interlocked healing rites begins. It's about two brothers visiting their father, the Sun, and then, later, killing the monsters that roam the earth.

That's an oversimplification, of course. But it clarifies some things that usually get lost in translation.

Elder Brother, Nayenezgani, for instance, in the midst of his heroic and demonic adventures, eats a snake. This proves to be his undoing. But he has this super sensitive brother, Tobachischin, to help him unravel the mysteries of disobedience. (As we know, you're not supposed to eat of the serpent!)

Elder Brother gets struck down by lightning … according to some ancient stories, he's shattered and put together again by the corn-carrying beetles, ant people and myriads of other creature helpers.

In the Navajo Ways, a person who has broken with tradition can fall into complete disharmony. Yet he can be healed and made whole again. In the prayers of old, the healing is a recitation of Elder Brother's return to wellness and power. To such a degree that he can heal others ... thus The Great Star Chant:

> *Nayenezgani returns with me through four white mists*
> *Whirling his dark staff about himself for protection, he re-*
> *turns with me*
> *With lightnings flashing behind him, with lightnings flashing*
> *before him*
> *He returns with me as the rainbow returns with me.*
> *Through mist and moss and blue clouds,*
> *As the rainbow returns, Nayenezgani returns with me.*

The flash of lightning is part of many myths and curing ceremonies. The animals and creatures that come with lightning "return" to aid the fallen, the sick, those in need of succor.

It is indeed lightning in the forefoot of Gila Monster. He is the first medicine man. Hummingbird came a little later. Gila Monster's also the earliest Hand Trembler. Then there's Bear with his fists of flint and lightning feet. Lightning comes with Great Snake, too. With his markings and way of traveling in circuitous zigs and zags and a kind of poetry of motion.

It was not long after I was struck by lightning that I had my own meeting with Great Snake. Later, too, I came in contact with a Star Person, who wore dark armor, and I had none.

Coyote men and star men came to the same council and I heard them and saw them and was stricken by them. But for the lightning in my bones, burned into my skull ... but for the sudden unforeseen appearance of Al-lan, the extraterrestrial who guided and protected Dr Frey while he lived and after he died, I might have fallen prey to evil and been paralyzed, and unable to tell this story.

But as Bluejay said to me once before, I live.

Chapter Four

Gila Monster was the first protective, as well as redemptive, medicine man. By calling forth his medicine, you can toughen your resistance to danger. You can reclaim your balance.

Gila Monster's origin story is called a "myth of armor".

This fits the big lizard's body type. He's well-armored with hard scales, a dark warrior of the creature kind. The original Hand Trembler. I've seen his left forefoot tremble. Especially when you wake him from his lair.

Ancient warrior tales speak of Gila Monster's strong physical defenses. His, so-called "flint armor".

However, he is, so the old tales tell us, a humorless guardian. He takes his job seriously—whatever guardianship he happens to have. He also punishes those who would mock him.

***

There is a story about Chipmunk, Watchman of the Corn. He doesn't take his job seriously. Gila Monster, they say, owns the corn field, but he sleeps during the day, and this is when Chipmunk, instead of watching over the corn, steals some, then a lot, to get in good with his mountain cousins.

What happens is this: Gila Monster catches the little thief and casts a spell on him. And this spell shrinks Chipmunk to the size of an ant.

As the story goes, Chipmunk begs forgiveness. Gila Monster, though gruff, is not mean. So he grants Chipmunk his freedom. He re-casts his spell, making Chipmunk normal size—all but his feet, which remain tiny to this day. "That is to remind you, Chipmunk, not to steal ever again." Those are the final words of Gila Monster when he restores Chipmunk.

I came to understand that Hand Trembling is a kind of lightning in the brain.

I experienced it when I was young. The time I got up from a nap and walked among the corn rows of our family farm. I liked to look for snakes and beetles and mice. That day as I remember, Ray, the farm hand put a dead copperhead snake around my neck.

Then he asked, "How's that for a necktie?"

To this day, sixty-five years later, I still recall the cold limp weight of that heavy snake. Its tail was twitching. "It's gonna do that until the sun goes down," Ray said.

Sure enough, when sundown came, the tail stilled.

But the snake vibration was yet in me, and my hand twitched.

I didn't know it then, but I was already, at age five, hand trembling.

I hand trembled, secretly, whenever there was a "moment" in my life that I couldn't explain. Whenever I was searching for something unknown. Whenever I was hurt or felt at odds with myself.

I still hand tremble when I want to know something. It comes on me when I haven't a direction, when I feel spiritually lost. Then the tremble comes and usually it points me to a story of some kind. One time it pointed me to several men in a cemetery. I'm going to explain that again later, but for now … the men were chanting over the fresh dug grave.

Their song was so entwined with the sun on cedars, with the four directions, and the sprinkling of corn pollen. In my mind, I again saw the dead copperhead. My living skin had become deeply acquainted with the serpent's dying skin. The trembling came later. Once I caught a wild bird and took it to bed with me and it fluttered madly to escape until I trembled over it and made it still. Then I released it to the cool summer air, and it flew away into the darkness.

My other close Navajo friend, Brown, told me that his aunt was a hand trembler. People came to her for help, for matters of divorce, financial trouble, ill health, and of course, spiritual matters.

"She used to boil bitterweed tea in back of her hogan. I still remember that smell like burnt copper. That old lady used to use rosary beads with her ceremonies and healings. She would make a person sit and thumb the beads, one by one, while saying Hail Marys.

"She told her patients they had to turn another direction of the compass after counting out seven beads. So she mixed her healings in certain ways with Navajo and Christian lore, but to tell you the truth, these medicines always worked. I never saw one that didn't, and I saw a lot of them. Rosaries and Hail Marys and old Auntie's left-hand twitching like a dead rattlesnake. You know that Elder Brother in the old stories eats a snake and falls sick, don't you?"

I told him I knew that story. "But I've never figured out how any of this stuff pulled off a healing unless it was all psychological."

"Everything is psychological," Brown said.

"Well," I asked, "How does the trembling work?"

Brown snorted the way he always did when someone was slow to figure out one of his lessons. "Look," he said, "If you want to get all-intellectual about it, "Auntie used to say that she went to an in-between place when she did her trance. You see, hand trembling isn't just wiggling your hand at the wind. It's a genuine expression of something from within, and you got to go to that in-between place to seek the cure for the person who is hurting, ailing, or whatever. One time I asked Auntie what the in-between place was like, and she said, 'It's a meadow up in the mountains.'

"I asked her if it was always that same place. She said, 'Sometimes I can't see it clearly. It's blurry. The way your eyes get when there's smoke in them. When that happens I have to wait until the trembling in my hand stops, and then starts up again fresh. When I see clearly it's always the same place: the grassy place between the mountains. There are sometimes elk up there, you know, Dzeeh, the great Bull Elk. He is a very good sign when he comes. Then I can see everything just so. The smoky tears must fall, then the mist goes away. I see him, Dzeeh, like I see you, now. After the mist clears, the trembling comes.'

"I asked her if that was the healing itself, or just the direction of the healing. She said, 'Both. Or neither.'

I told Brown that when I was on the farm and did the tremble, usually after I went to bed, it always put me to sleep.

He said, "I bet you had some pretty weird dreams."

Then he snorted like a bull elk.

Chapter Five

I noticed the nurse's tattoo when she took my blood pressure.

"May I see that more closely?" I asked.

She rolled up her sleeve. Now I was the nurse interviewing the nurse.

"What gave you the idea to have a grandfather clock on your arm?"

The clock was very ornate, many-colored, beautifully detailed.

She shook her head, smiled, "I thought I was asking the questions," she said. "Well, since you asked first, this clock was my grandmother's. She meant all the world to me, to us, our family. When she was dying, the grandfather clock was at ten of twelve."

"The one on your arm is at midnight," I commented.

"Yes, it is. She died at midnight and her clock stopped."

"Just like that?"

"At exactly that hour. And that was exactly when her heart stopped. I was there. I know."

She then proceeded to ask me some questions. "Where are you living presently? Where did you live previously? What do you do?"

"I thought I answered those questions on the form from the insurance company."

She smiled. "Your wife did. You didn't."

"Well, we live at The Veranda apartments on Sawmill in Santa Fe. Originally, we lived in Tesuque, and after our daughters went to college we moved to a barrier island in Florida and we also lived in Jamaica."

"Why is your blood pressure so high?" she questioned.

"I guess I am agitated."

"May I ask why?"

"Well, our truck was stolen last night. A person committed suicide in our apartment complex. And someone is trying to kill someone in the apartment next door to us."

"That would explain it," she said. "You're 140 0ver 90."

I chuckled. "Does that mean my grandfather clock is ten to twelve."

She made a face. "Not exactly." Then she smiled again. "The doctor will see you in a minute. Remember to tell him that you were struck by lightning."

I often forgot about that.

But what I really wanted to tell her was this: Everything I'd said was true. I'd spent the morning hand trembling, watching my hand. Checking to see which way my fingers pointed.

After a while, my hand trembled toward the south.

So I knew our truck was going in that direction.

Hand trembling raises the pressure.

But it also points the way.

***

Laura and I had not talked about Al-lan for years. But this night, the darkness, the lost truck, stirred up all kinds of things from our present and our past.

We were sitting on our apartment balcony at The Veranda looking toward the parking lot where only hours before our truck was safely parked.

"And you looked everywhere?" she asked.

"Absolutely everywhere. Every lot on the grounds. It's just not here. It has to be stolen."

The sky was beginning to grow grey. Morning was maybe an hour away. The air had a hint of rain and that brought back the memory of Al-lan. We didn't talk about it at first.

There was this hollow feeling of desolation. And grief, because that old F150 truck had gotten us through so many hurricanes, snowstorms, dust-devils, floods, scrapes of all kinds.

We went back to that time in the Everglades, lost and alone, just the two of us. We'd parked beside a bog full of gators. I had a road map spread out but it didn't help. We were off a main road on a wiggly worm path, so lost we couldn't read a map. But we felt somewhat safe in the truck. I looked at the gas gauge. Almost empty.

I had just finished a hand trembling.

Which way? Which way? I asked the endless, croaking dark.

My left arm slowly raised.

My index finger quivered.

I peered into the darkness.

Laura said, "There! You see it?"

My eye followed my finger.

"Yes!"

There in the swamp gloom was a red Buddha sitting on a stone.

Behind the Buddha there was the faint glimmer of an almost unseen road.

We turned the truck around ever so slowly—the road was very narrow and the gators watched out of the steam rising from the bog. I wrestled the wheel and turned the truck toward the glimmer-road. It required me to drive along the edge of the swamp. The frogs boomed. The gators barked. Slowly, we squooshed past the Buddha and the bog and made it through a tangle of palmettos and mangroves to the hard sand road that eventually meandered to the Tamiami Trail. Beyond that, the glitter of Miami.

I went back and bowed to the Buddha and kissed the old truck.

That night, well past Fakahatchee Strand, into the emptiness of sawgrass, Laura took the wheel, and an hour before we got to the Airboat Park, we struck a root in the road that turned out to be the biggest rattler either of us had ever seen. Well over eight feet. There was swamp lightning bouncing off bushes that night and sometimes it looked like something else.

"Laura, did you see that?"

"It looked like a plane, but it was bright white."

"I think it was a lightning strike."

A moment after it hit, a man came limping along by the side of the road.

More like a scarecrow than a man.

Laura stopped the truck and the man got into the back seat smelling of burnt rubber and fish.

"What happened?" I asked him.

"Road trouble."

I turned to have a better look at him. He was gaunt, ragged, dripping wet.

"Lose your car?" I asked.

"Lost everything," he said.

"Is your … family … all right?"

"Haven't any to speak of."

"Where were you coming from?" Laura asked.

The wind was wailing.

Rain drumming down in miasmic twists and spirals.

Lightning lit the interior of the truck.

I heard a groan and looked behind me.

The wasted-faced, crumpled man was gone.

In his place there was a soaking wet, whining dog.

Chapter Six

"The dog jumped out of the truck at Miccosukee Air Boat Park," Laura said.

It was nearly sunup and we were sipping piñon roast coffee and talking about the night in the Everglades. Here and now, the cemetery on the other side of the coyote fence north of The Veranda was suffused with melon-colored light. The sacred moment of sun was spreading out like a great blanket of beauty. Inside the apartment a single blade of sunlight touched Jay's painting of the corn mothers.

"That dog," I said to Laura, "we never saw him again."

The golden dawn spread farther into the lowland heather. The dark trees shone with light on one side and dark on the other.

The parking place where the truck had been parked looked empty, and as I imagined, accusatory.

It was my own damn fault. I should've parked it down by the gym where the cops parked.

We sat in silence, thinking. The window was open and we could smell the dawn.

Laura said, "But why did we imagine that beaten down guy was Al-lan?"

I laughed. "Are you imagining Al-lan stole our truck?"

"More likely, the dog stole it."

"The dog drives cars? According to Dr Frey, Al-lan had a lot of trouble with automobiles."

"On his planet, terrestrial vehicles just jump over obstacles."

"Obstacles being stop signs and red lights and other vehicles on our planet."

Laura took a sip of coffee. "I always thought the dog was Al-lan."

"Then who was the man?"

"The man was the dog." She smiled, sipped, kept smiling.

"Seriously," I added, "there would need to be someone inside this apartment building … someone who stayed awake all night and told someone else on the other side of the fence when the coast was clear."

I lowered my voice to an even softer whisper. "You know, the guy next to us in Apartment 1804?"

Laura's lips tightened. "You mean the man who beats his daughter?"

"What I hear coming through the wall isn't beating."

"What then?"

I narrowed my eyes. "You're kidding, right?"

She stared at me.

"He's fucking his daughter, not beating her," I said.

Laura stood up from her chair looked out at the fingers of yellow light on the wet grass. The sprinklers were on and there were little rivulets running downhill from the upper parking lot. The morning sun was silvering these ribbons of running water. The morning beckoned but so did our conversation.

She sat down. "That's terrible," she said. "They're disgusting, all of them. There's the teen girl who wears her long straight hair down in front of her face, god knows how she can see anything but apparently she does. There's the mom, if she is a mom, with her fat butt, her leotards and her stupid tutu. And the man … that little short stub clown of a man with his square head and those dead *pinche madre* eyes."

That was the most fluent and funny text out of Laura's mouth in quite a while. Her silence was sometimes a blessing, sometimes a curse, but when she spoke lines like that I really listened.

"They're beyond weird, those three. They're escapees … from something."

"We're leaving out the little boy," she reminded.

"Oh, right. How could I forget that little shit? Caught him pissing off the balcony yesterday."

"—You stop him?"

"Antonio, the yard man, did. The kid was literally pissing on Antonio's golf hat."

"You mean, head."

17

"Hat and head."

I sighed, took a last sip of smoky coffee. "We ought to get out of this place."

Laura gave me another stare. "We just got here."

"We can't exactly leave without our truck. I can't carry all our stuff on my back."

Her soft sarcasm baited me a little more. "If Al-lan returns we can get him to move our stuff. After all, he has powers."

"Powers schmowers," I said. "It's time to call the cops and report our missing truck."

"Did you do your trembling? That might help."

"I did that already. My left hand pointed south."

"Do it again. Meanwhile I'll call the police station."

I went into the bathroom.

I liked to tremble, and travel, barefoot in the tub.

Chapter Seven

When Laura got off the phone, I got out of the tub.

"I spoke to the detective," she said, "you know, the one who is taking the case. He said there have been three stolen vehicles here at The Veranda. Someone stripped a new Jeep, took the roof rack, the bumpers, tires, and left the vehicle on blocks. You've met the guy who lives downstairs named Mick?"

"You mean the oil field worker from Texas who's a Kaw Indian?"

Laura said, "Same one. Apparently he drinks a lot, has a bad temper. The Detective Archuleta said Mick is furious because he thinks the same thief stole his Corvette. He has three cars out there in the parking lot and the Vette is the one he loves. So that's gone … oh, and a new computer was ripped off, too. A laptop taken right off a woman's kitchen table while she was doing dishes."

"So what hope did the detective give you?"

Laura shook her head. "Not much. He said he's driving around, looking for a 1993 F150. There aren't too many of those old classics around, are there?"

I nodded. "While I was trembling in the tub I saw some visions. The old truck was getting a beating in a wallow down by the Santa Fe river. Or maybe it was somewhere around La Cienega. I'm pretty sure the crook had repainted it black. I mean spray painted, really awful. It had welts and dents, too."

"That doesn't sound like our truck. It was new looking."

"Was," I said. "Who knows, maybe I saw something happening in Mexico."

"Well," Laura said, "the detective thinks he might've seen our truck here, somewhere on Richards Avenue. It was last night and the driver was going fast and just disappeared. He was out of the uniform and couldn't make an arrest, but he said he was on the case and would do some more searching today."

Suddenly there was a terrible banging in 1804 the apartment next door.

"*Open up, you sonufabitch*, I got something for you."

It was the Kaw man, Mick. He was known to carry a pistol and I saw it now by peering over the edge of our balcony. The door opened. Mick, dressed in black, was tall and about as hard-edged as a man could be. Probably in his fifties but all sinew and leather, and loaded for action. The gun was a Glock and he had it pointed towards the door, and then the door opened wide.

The diminutive man in the doorway was square looking, but almost shoulderless. His mouth was pursed and wide like a bullfrog's. His eyes were deep set and glittery, and they gleamed at Mick. A wet smile slipped across his frog face.

Laura and I stood there, watching. A moment frozen in time.

Then, when Mick rammed his gun into the guy's ribs, I whispered to Laura, "Call your detective."

She left. I stood there, witness to what I thought was going to be a murder.

Mick spoke to the frog man. "I'll blow those smug rubber lips to hell," he said. "You're a goddamned thief and you don't come out of here except at night, and I know that because I've been watching you, motherfucker."

I imagined frog face might be mute. But then he suddenly bellowed with such volume that Mick took a step backward.

"Put your gun away, old man," the guy roared, "or I'll be forced to kill you."

And then, a second later, he raised his hands, palms open.

Instantly, Mick fell back, as if he were made of wet paper.

The fat frog laughed, a muffled chortle.

Then, broken by what appeared to be an invisible blow, Mick crawled over to where I was standing in astonishment and began thumping his gun handle against the base of our metal door. "Let me in, Let me in," he said in a hoarse voice.

The round-shouldered frog ninja smiled. Then seeing Mick incapacitated, he turned, slowly walked to his apartment door, opened it and softly stepped inside.

I helped Mick up but he waved me away and went down the stairs like a shadow.

Laura met me at our door. "The detective was out but two cops are on their way now. What happened? There was a lot of noise out here."

"You wouldn't believe it if I told you. I'm not even sure I saw it myself."

I told her what had happened.

Moments later, the cops arrived.

Two dark blue dandies in spotless uniforms. The woman was pretty, not tall but straight-shouldered. She was black haired and fine featured. Her partner was equally a central casting type. Both spoke softly and clearly. After briefly questioning us, they walked over to 1804 and knocked on the metal door.

From where we stood on our balcony, we could see our blocky neighbor holding off the officers. The strange man was polite but firm. And he yielded not an inch.

"We need to see your identification," the lady cop said. "Driver's license, please."

"Don't have one," the frog-lipped man said.

"Show us whatever identification you have," the male cop ordered.

"Haven't any." He gave them a broad smile that revealed a mouthful of gray teeth.

"We'll have to come in then," the male policeman said.

He edged into the doorway and his partner followed him.

After they were in the door closed with a click.

We waited in our living room, certain that they'd take the weirdo away.

They didn't. We heard argumentation. But no violence.

The cops came out and went directly to our door.

They seemed less confident than before. "What happened?" I asked.

"Do you wish to make a complaint?" the woman asked.

Laura and I shook our heads. "Not really," she said. "But we would like to know who, or what, those people are."

"So would we," the male cop said. The woman nodded, then said, "There's a family in there. The wife's the only one with any identification.

21

The girl is sort of faceless with all that hair hanging down. The wife stands there like a post and says nothing while the husband does all the talking. We need to find out who they are and where they came from."

"The rumor around here is that the man only recently got out of prison," Laura said. "That's one rumor, the other one is that the guy got into some trouble with the mafia and they're looking for him."

"Hence, no ID," the man mentioned.

"You couldn't arrest them?" I asked.

"For what?" the man said. "It sounds like this neighbor of yours, Mick, threatened them with a gun."

"That is true," I said. "He did that. But there have been a bunch of car thefts here in the last 24 hours and—"

She cut me off. "There's nothing we can do about that until we have more information. But, I promise you, we will investigate these folks and find out who they are. And we'll let you know. In the meantime, keep your doors locked and don't antagonize them. They're pretty easily provoked."

"We've heard some peculiar noises coming from that apartment over there," Laura said.

"What kind of noises?" the woman asked.

"What I would call, well, sexual sounds," Laura replied.

"That's not necessarily against the law," the male cop said with a small whisper of a smile.

"It is if there's a minor involved with an adult who could be her father," Laura said sharply.

The cop sighed. "Have you any proof of this? You will need something provable, something like a tape recording. Then, we could run tests and see if the voices match up to the people across the landing."

"This all sounds like a sting operation," Laura said, shaking her head. "We're not detection experts and we don't have expensive recording equipment."

Both cops shrugged, glanced meaningfully at each other, then the woman said, "All right. We have to go. Be back in touch when we find out something about your neighbors."

As they were leaving, I said, "Didn't you find those people to be, more than a little bit odd?"

"He means creepy," Laura said.

Both of them smiled indulgently and said, "Have a good day."

Chapter Eight

However, it wasn't a good day.

Have you ever loved something inanimate?

I mean in the sentimental way a child loves a stuffed blue dog? Or a panda bear?

That's the way we felt about our missing truck.

That beloved maroon metal beast had gotten us through seven hurricanes in Florida. It had survived side rolls in deep mosquito ditches. It had been battered by flying bass during a category 5. Not flying fish—fish driven through the air like missiles. It had witnessed, as I had witnessed, a carpenter's level that the wind had picked up in some distant vicinity and had planted into an almond tree. The F150 had been a partner, a pal of the world, in some of the worst situations on earth.

Once, I had parked it in front of the garage door during the onset of Hurricane Charley. I nosed it, so to say, right up against the door. The metal garage door was nudged into the two steel channels that held it in place. And thus we spent the night in the lightless garage amongst our many books in boxes and on shelves.

Somehow we had no doubt the truck would stay where I'd lodged it, and with its chrome grille grinning, we hunkered down and listened to the wailing wind. The keening maniacal wind that took down every telephone pole on the barrier island. That deadly whining, deep-throated wind that destroyed hundreds of homes. Only crazy people, suicidals, stayed on-island for the final shootout, which happened after the quiet, sunshiny eye, passed over our roof.

We were among those crazies—Laura and I and our two Great Danes, our Siamese cat, our two iridescent Malaysian sharks, and our forty-year-old blue-fronted parrot, George, who'd been with us since our children, now grown with children of their own, were born. All of us—people, animals, birds and books—made it through.

In magical thinking there is no logic. The truck, we believed, saved us.

But across the street at our neighbor's house it wasn't so pretty. When the sun came back his giant travel trailer lay crushed on its side. Underneath that behemoth was his mother's new blue Cadillac.

Miraculously, our F-150 looked like it had gone to a car wash. Not a scratch. Fifteen feet from where the truck was parked a 160-foot Madagascar Ear Tree had crashed down, sealing off every household door except the garage.

Ah, yes. We remember hurricanes. Hurucan, the Carib god of fury.

Twenty years later and seven hurricanes behind us, the truck is stolen. We are back in New Mexico with George, the same place where we started out, where Laura and I met, actually. But no truck. The morning after the theft, I cried. So did she. And then we went out to face the day. Truckless, luckless, clueless as to what to do. We hadn't the money to even buy a bicycle.

But we did have enough change for coffee and a donut at Dunkin. We went there and did that thing. And, as it happened, I saw something silly that cheered us up and made us laugh. I wrote it down on a napkin:

Symptom and Sign at Dunkin …

The sign read—Athrooms for paying customers only! Ath first, we give you key! No sleeping. No vaping.

We laughed hard at that and meanwhile a dust devil boiled up out of the cemetery across from Dunkin and tossed plastic flowers around the graves.

The man sitting next to us shouted, Caliente! into his coffee cup. I said to Laura, "Either his coffee is talking to him or he's mad at it for being hot." He lowered his head and whispered secrets not meant for this world to his coffee cup. "Dulce, dulce," he said. And, "Bueno, bueno."

I said to Laura, "Ath me no question, me tell you no lie."

"Maybe his coffee could tell us where our truck is," Laura said.

***

Back at The Veranda, I saw Mick under the parking portal working on his 1965 Jaguar with the twelve-cylinder engine. The hood was always up on that long torpedo thing, and we never saw him driving it.

"Sorry about your truck," he said. "Sorry about banging on your door. I went nuts when I heard about your truck and decided to even the score. I am ready even now to kill the fucker." He patted his black sweatshirt. Mick smiled crookedly and shook his head. "Them people have shit for brains. I think the old man, you know the dwarf dad, is fucking that young girl with the long hair."

"How do you figure?"

"I figure the lady that lives down from you, Gabriela, you know the Cuban woman, she's a bonafide psychic, and she knows who's fucking and who's just plain fucked up, know what I mean. She's the one heard them going at it night before last. He does it standing, she says. You hear all kinds of noises up there. Down where I live it's quieter unless them Filipinos have a go at it. They throw china dishes at each other. That can get expensive."

He looked me in the eye while he wiped the Jaguar grease off his hands. He was a handsome man, high-cheek-boned, trim white bearded with a long pale pony tail woven nicely in back. He had sky blue eyes and his skin was reddish in the sun. He looked Indian, if you squinted at him in a certain way, and didn't know what Indians looked like.

I stood there with Laura listening to Mick and watching him check the compression on the Jag that wouldn't run unless it was motionless in the parking lot. He'd had it on one good long run down to Socorro and then it was garaged and he had to take the bus back. So much for '65 Jags.

I thought to myself: If you could shake the night-weary thought of your loss, you might love this beautiful New Mexico day. It was March and the new leaves were just appearing on the elders and elms. The cottonwoods were greening up, too. There was a caw of crows in the sky and a rasp of ravens in the junipers. The whimsy of some warblers on the portal beams.

"Those ravens," Mick said. "They're making some plans. Hear 'em? They got something up their sleeve all right."

"Maybe they're planning to gang up and peck the eyes out of those weirdos in Apartment 1804."

Mick chuckled. "I ever introduce you to Teresina?"

"That your girlfriend?"

"Yes, indeed," Mick said.

A beautiful young woman raised her head over the side of the bullet-shaped, hood-lifted, silver Jag. She, too, looked native. But there was something funny going on in her eyes, like she wasn't much behind them. A sadder face I've never seen.

We introduced ourselves. She offered me the softest hand I've never felt, so to say, and I thought I saw a tiny tear in her eye.

"Couldn't do nothin' without my Teresina," Mick said, picking up a wrench and having another go at the engine, which was almost as long as the Jag itself. No, it was actually longer, to my eye, anyway.

Mick said, "What kinda dog is that you've got there?"

"Dog?" I said. Laura and I both glanced around. There was a black cat slinking toward the coyote fence. No dog anywhere we could see.

"Looks to be Chow with some retriever," Mick commented, his head buried in engine musk and oil and valves and ....

"I love them dogs," Mick said. He was deep into the engine cavity. As if sort of swimming in there with his engineer boot soles sticking out, his legs and body like a diving board, flat out.

"Where did you see a dog?" Laura asked.

Teresina gave us the faintest wisp of smile. She handed Mick a silver socket wrench. "Mick sees things we don't."

"Yeah, I love them dogs," he said again. "Don't you?"

"If I could see 'em," I said.

"I hear your parrot sometimes," he added. "Sounds like a real talkative fellow."

"You could say that again," Laura mentioned.

"Do you ever see things that aren't there?" I asked Mick.

"All the time."

He came away from the engine. "I see ghosts that are there, though, and dogs that aren't, I guess. Seriously, now, where'd that dog go to, anyway? It was a purple tongue chow, for sure. Bite you every time."

Chapter Nine

The disappearing dog …

I flashed on that creepy dismal night in the Everglades.

There was the strange man, then no man.

Then the dog. The wet dog with the purple tongue.

Did I just say that?

Slippery memories make you think of slippery times. Slippery times make you …

… try the bathtub tremble to see if you can conjure a dog with a purple tongue.

But nothing came to the porcelain, pill chamber, the space craft of many nightly journeys into mind and matter, and sometimes, into places of neither.

Time to get out of the tub and do some honest fact checking.

So that night Laura and I visited Gabriela, the mystic woman who lived one floor down from us.

Gabriela met us at the door with a gracious smile. She was really a lovely woman, the lightest skin Cuban, a red tint to her hair, green-blue eyes, a strong body that she explained right off was beset with rheumatoid arthritis.

"I have to sleep more than most people, rest more than I want to, and conduct my life from a couch, a bed, and, well … it gets worse from there. I take a lot of pills for pain and for reduction of bone inflammation, but none of this has anything to do with your visit … how can I help, other than say how sorry I am your pretty truck got stolen and some dirty thief has probably sold it across the river in Mission, Texas or some other stop gap town that our president wants to wall off, or wall in, but that's beside the point, or is it?"

She took a large breath and continued in the same manner, running on and off and saying other things about how she liked my turquoise ring and Laura's silver earrings and my cowboy hat and her husband Jeff was there smiling all the while and nodding and adding special facial effects as the storyteller's assistant. We hardly got a word in edgewise, which was OK, because what we really wanted to know was what Gabriela knew about the people upstairs.

Did she think they were involved in any of the mounting thefts on the apartment complex? Was the dwarf guy a plant who checked the parking lot and made calls when he saw vehicles that were undriven, or otherwise unused for days on end? Did she think the girl was being raped by her father? What did she think of the woman of the house? Mother? Friend? Accomplice?

Gabriela drew a deep breath. Her eyes widened.

She said, "In answer to all your questions, they're guilty as charged, that is to say, for every crime on these premises. I did a check on the man whose name is Appleplum; did you ever hear of a person named that? No? Sounds made-up, doesn't it? Well, I can tell you, his past is invisible to us. He began to exist, so to speak, in 1995, but there's nothing on him on the internet, or on my psychic screen, except an implication that he was involved in a crime of some sort in Arizona, was arrested here and sentenced to a jail term in Espanola Federal where he got out on good behavior and has been involved in uncertain and devious felonies ever since, and yes, he's a plant for someone or some thing, and his wife, too, I should suppose, and the daughter is banged every night, I hear them and Jeff hears them, too, and we bang back on the ceiling and sometimes they quiet down but most of the time they go at it even louder and with more bumping and grinding, such a little man with maybe such a big tool, as we say, and there you have it, except for the little boy who is probably innocent as most little boys unless he's passing piss in ziplock bags and then throwing them at the heads of passerbys, and such, mail people have yelled bloody murder at the little prick, but mostly he stays quiet, but have you heard him talk?"

I said, "well, actually I—" But she cut me off and rolled on like the Columbia River in a rainstorm, saying, "It's the girl I worry about, I've called the Courtesy Police, the Santa Fe Police, Children's Protective Services, and a local detective agency (too expensive) and all anyone'll say is come back when you have a video or a recording of what's going on up there, we need to hear and see it and believe it otherwise it's nothing, even though we are inclined to believe what you're saying because we've had other calls of a similar nature."

"I think, we think that—"

"I know what you mean," Gabriela said. Look, if you want to know what to do, you're the closest to those creeps, you should be able to hear them when they go at it at night. Do you have any recording equipment, we have to catch them in the act and it's important to get the girl's voice in there, the one we hear down at this lower level, she is making all kinds of orgasmic noises."

"Any chance that …" I looked her in the eye and sent her a telepathic message, LET ME SPEAK, and she got very quiet, resettled comfortable on the couch and gave me the sweetest, prettiest smile, and said, "Continue, please."

"Any chance that it's the girl doing, well, everything?"

Gabriela laughed. "That's good for a story, but I don't think so. From the grunts and groans we hear down here (Jeff made a vaudevillian face) it's all coming from the man, you listen and you'll hear—"

I butted in with my mind and cut her off with telepathy whereupon she smiled and nodded for me to continue.

"It sounds like the guy's lifting weights," I said. "My grandson and I heard him when we were walking on the path last night, real gorgon-like burst, of UH and AH, AHRGH. Short staccato noises like that, the kind you hear at the gym down the hill, the gym, I might add, that he never goes to."

"Same sounds we hear," Jeff put in. Everyone turned to look at him. He had a mellow tone to his voice, it was good and smooth and could convince anyone of anything. "We hear him," he said with emphasis.

"And he's jerking off standing up," Gabriela said loudly. "No question about it."

"We are supposed to record this vile crap," Laura said, shaking her head.

Gabriela smiled. Her crafty green eyes danced. Then she laughed.

"It's Bad Boy Scout Camp, I agree, but men do make those sounds when they complete a hand-job, right, Jeff?"

He nodded, raised his eyebrows, shook his head. "Don't record that, if you don't want to."

"Is it considered a sex act if the daughter is just watching?"

"I'll look that up," Gabriela said, "but, say, any word on your truck?"

At that moment, Laura's cell made some insistent cricket chirps.

Chapter Ten

Alan Watts once said, "There is a thing called spontaneous action or marvelous activity. You can't aspire to it. It happens."

So when we say, "shit happens" do we negate the good and accentuate the bad?

From a purely Zen point of view, I believe we do neither. Which is why we like to say, shit happens. It just naturally does. Unmotivated. Unprovoked. Marvelous activity in retrograde. Dystopia in full flower.

Imagine: seagulls flying backward from the beckoning sea. Waves in contradiction, reversing direction. Everything going backward. The mad March Hare's very merry unbirthday.

Well, something like this was happening to me, to us, to the whole world. True, I'd stopped crying over spilt truck oil. I missed the bright new tailgate my cousin Peter had put on the truck, the blazing gold and white lights that lit up the night, the comfortable, easy feel of friendship the truck imparted. But shit happens, good shit and bad shit. We were without wheels for no more than a couple days when my brother's wife announced she was getting a new car, would we like her old one? A Subaru with 200,000 miles on it, but as they say here in Santa Fe, a Suby's good for 300,000 thousand or more.

We took the 2001 Subaru, wholly and gladly, and when we offered our sister-in-law cash, she refused. So we now had a free and clear car, but that night more shit happened. There were several more robberies, but I forgot to say that Mick got his Vette back. He did some hand trembling of his own. His hand pointed south, and he went to Espanola.

In front of an old service station, parked behind a tower of discarded tires, Mick's Vette glittered in the dark. He saw it, called the police. They told him he could take the vehicle but he had to prove he was the rightful owner. This required a trip to the DMV, another trip back to Espanola, and Mick repossessed his Vette only to find out that his girlfriend, Teresina, had tried to take her life. Fortunately, she'd failed in her attempt—a bottle of gin and near drowning in her bathtub—and now Mick was looking after her.

Mercury was in retrograde and there was a sallow March mad moon hanging over us, but Laura and I felt better because Detective John Archuleta was on the trail of our F150. He had seen it and said he knew where it lived. Another day and he would have a warrant for the arrest of the thief.

We went to bed that night feeling that, well, shit happens, but there's also "marvelous action" that preempts a shitfall, and makes for a kind of calm. In Jamaica they say, "Walk good." In Zen they say, "When walking, just walk."

I was sleepwalking though when I heard mice singing under the sink. I found them, too. A whole tribe of little brown house mice. Singing! In harmony, it sounded like. I never knew mice could sing, did you? Well, when they saw my incredulous face, they shut up and ran for it.

I went back to bed. Some shit happening that was.

Laura was deep asleep, so she missed the concert. However, there was new one.

Through the adobe walls I now heard a dithyramb, a bacchanal fantasy sex fest—or whatever you want to call it. I heard The Girl, as we'd come to call her, singing. Tutu, as we'd come to call her, was stomping. The big kahoona, Appleplum, was chortling like a baby beluga. But where was The Boy?

We'd heard him that same afternoon saying to Tutu, "Well, it comes to my attention that the plants will grow even when the sidewalk blocks their passage. They will grow and grow until they burst through their cement impediment, and Spring starts anew!"

So where was The Boy? Watching from his bed?

Imagination is a terrible thing.

Equal to beauty in awesome destructiveness.

Now, Laura has the gift of deepest sleep, I don't. I decided to get up and go out for a breath of fresh air. As I passed the neighbor's window, I noticed a tiny part in the curtain. A quick glance. Tutu's bare butt flashed like a silver moon. It was that big, though cracked. Appleplum was wiping himself dry with a towel, and I wish I hadn't seen either of those two.

But The Girl … I allowed myself to take a quick blink at her nakedness. It would not be far off to say she was something out of Maxfield Parrish. Not yet fully developed, but what was there was beautiful. One blink of someone passing for no more than a second, but she saw me seeing her and smiled faintly at the revelation.

I hastened quickly, dazedly, down the stairs and into the New Mexico March night of popping trees.

And almost tripped over …

… Mick's bite-you-every-time dog.

Chapter Eleven

"Hello, there," I said to the dog.

"How's it going up there?" the dog said.

"Who said that?" I said.

"I did," the dog said.

I had not had but one draw of herb before I left the apartment. Not enough to give a dog a voice like Noel Coward.

The dog was a shepherd, black and glossy, with fetlocks of wisp. Practically a show dog. I say practically, because it had lots of gross burrs. But be that as it may, this was a beautiful animal, and then again, why shouldn't it speak, being so beautiful, and why shouldn't it have its share of burry fur? The dark spaniel-like eyes were incredible—what, on earth was behind that too-innocent, more than mild intelligent gaze?

I have always believed animals could talk. This one was talking with its eyes.

And speaking words into my inner ear.

The dog said, "I see that you are at one remove. Is it that I can talk?"

"Well, maybe," I replied. "How do I know this isn't an illusion, some auditory phenomena, a bit of undigested cheese, as old Mister Scrooge once said. "

"You don't," the dog said. "There's no apparent logic here. Not human-logic anyway. And you humans are extremely fussy and fixated on keeping your animals on the logic-leash. Talking's therefore quite out of bounds for canines."

"Let's play the logic game, then," I put in. "How about you prove to me you're really a talking dog. By the way, if this is just going on inside my head, that's OK, too."

"It most definitely is," the dog said, sitting down on the grass. A play of moonlight and a breath of crosswind made its fur gleam. The large moist eyes were on me, as were, I felt, its thoughts.

"All right," the dog said. "Point one, I do pass my thoughts directly into the channels of your right brain. What you hear is a simulated voice, so I am like your female map genie, Siri, who speaks in very clear tones."

"I am reading you, loud and clear."

"Would you like me to lower my voice?"

But before I could answer, the dog struck a familiar pose, leg lifted, head down, and bit at a flea, or perhaps a legion of fleas. "Your planet is a vast flea farm, which makes it inconvenient for me. On the other hand, I mean paw, you people are very easy to read, so I rarely do much talking."

"Once again, please, how the hell do I know I am not making all this up? I do that, you know. I am a writer by trade. I make stuff up, professionally, and this little confab is right now inspiring a story."

The dog's flea circus seemed to be at bay, as it were. It sat poised and composed and resumed its neutral but earnest stare.

Suddenly, without warning, it jumped up and wrapped its paws around me. It was a genuine hug, a human-like embrace. Still, I staggered backward. The dog was strong.

"Down!" I said, in an authoritative voice.

The dog dropped to all fours, and said: "Let me define that for you. Let's see, DOWN: an undulating, usually treeless, upland expanse of grasses. DOWN: a lower physical position, which is probably the definition you intended here. But you might've meant, because of the physical action a DOWN, as in the game of football. Or perhaps you meant to say DOWN, as in depressed or dejected, but you don't seem to be that type. You could've meant DOWN, as in 'I am down with that, meaning that you like doggy hugs. Lastly, and most remotely, you wanted to express the softness of my fur, as if it were like a bird's DOWN. I'm quite certain you didn't mean DOWN, as in lower the price. Am I right?"

I took another step back, and in doing so, I remembered Etienne, the mage who could leave his body and astral project himself into space, telling me that Al-lan, the extraterrestrial, could tremble himself into human bodies and thus impart information to them without seeing him.

Was this unpredictable dog none other than Al-lan?

No sooner did I think that, the dog jumped up, hugged me again. This time I didn't fall away or push it away. "Have I guessed correctly then?"

The dog said, "You can call me Al-lan."

Chapter Twelve

"Al-lan can you help me find my truck?"

He looked at me curiously. The wind ruffled his dog feathers.

He licked himself a couple of times, very busily, noisily.

Then looked back at me. "Truth is," he said, "I don't really like being a dog, but it's much easier than being human. We are all sparks of light from the heavens, that much I know. There are bands, declinations of time and space, call them leitmotifs, if you will. They play in the universe, light and dark, by turns, kind of like Wagner's Valkyries, they come and go. But whether you see them or not, they are there. I came, I come, from one of those leitmotifs."

"Is it a planet?"

"That's much too simple. You've heard of dark matter?"

I scratched my head, remembering Neil deGrasse Tyson's book, *Astrophysics for People in a Hurry*. Dark Matter: sort of like holes in the universe. Holes where things happen, but science can't define what dark matter holes do except they seem not to have gravity, yet they draw planetary bodies, stars and such, to them. They have an unknown power.

"Dark matter draws things to it."

Al-lan nodded. "I come from such a place."

"Is it dark there?"

"Not really."

"But it cannot be seen."

"That is correct."

"Look," he said, "Let's get your truck back. Or some semblance of it."

"That sounds like magic."

Al-lan laughed, in a doggy kind of way. It sounded a little like choking.

"There's no so-called magic in the universe," he said, and shook his ears so that they flapped and made a leathery sound.

"The best we can do is find the truck, see where it is, and in what kind of shape it's in, and then maybe we can coax it back."

"How do we do that?" I asked.

"I don't know yet. You're the hand trembler. Have you trembled the truck?"

"It's in a dark place, heading south, I think."

Al-lan sniffed the grass. "It smells like mint at night," he said. "That is one thing I like about being canine. The smells are six-dimensional."

"Is that going to get us to the truck?"

"No. But you can tremble yourself into me, and find out better than I can where the truck is."

"If I go into you, Al-lan, where will you be?"

"I'll be here, waiting."

I scratched my head again. "In what form? How will I recognize you?"

"You will feel me more than see me. We'll switch when our feeling is strongest. Don't worry, that part is easiest. Getting into me is a little bit harder, but then I am not a trembler and you are. Maybe it will be a piece of cake for you."

"So when do we make the exchange or whatever it is?"

"How about now?"

"What about Laura? Should I go upstairs and tell her I am leaving?"

Al-lan made the choking noise again.

"You're not going far, my friend. And it may only take seconds. Time has no fixed abode. It's not a commodity like you think. It isn't anything, really."

"Then let's do it."

No sooner had I said it than it was done. I was out of my body and into his. I was all dog, complete with wagging tail and salivating mouth and … the smells! He was so right. They came at me like a thousand bulldozers. They beckoned and bombasted. They ploughed through the courts of night, turning everything over. I couldn't move—except for my tail—the scents of earth and sky overwhelmed me, inundated my mind.

Al-lan, as he'd said, was somewhere else, in something else. I couldn't see him or hear him. How could I tremble, given that I had paws and not hands? But the answer to that came quickly. My whole body was suddenly a-tremble. From my quivering nose to my vibrating tail, I was having a kind of trembler seizure. I lay down, paws in front of me, tail flat out, nose to the wind.

Almost immediately, I smelled truck. I trembled all over upon the scent of its familiarity. And then, still humming bodily, I found myself in the back of my F150. I lay down again, feeling the hard rubber bed cover against my chest. I was nearly invisible. The truck was full of baling wire rolls, bumpers, cables, tailgates, steering wheels, backseats, tires and all kinds of unnamable trash, some of which was old newspaper blowing, at cyclonic intervals, out over the bed and into the starry night.

Now and again, a head would appear in the back window. A shaven hillbilly head, complete with Billy Bob teeth. Two others were in the front seat. I could see their shadowy heads, too. But the weird thing was the guy looking back all the time couldn't see me. Oh, then I realized … I had the blackest fur and I was lying flat and not moving and there was junk all around me, even a swatch of old green canvas that kept trying to take flight from one end of the bed to the other.

When the truck stopped in a dry riverbed. I reversed my position and hopped out. Then I took cover behind a barricade of chamisa. The louts got out. One of them had a sledge hammer, the other guy from the front seat had a can of spray paint. Baldy from the back seat had a rat-tail file, a lug wrench, and that was about all I could see, but, my god, the smells.

I could pick up everything from owl barf to coyote shit and from cryptogamic grass (and that ancient stuff isn't supposed to have an odor) to chamisa roots. I got a scent of these guys' sweaty boots and unchanged underwear, and then as I was wallowing in this nose-worthy feast of the senses, there came some unimaginable sounds. I realized then that Al-lan had left out the ear part—because I now could hear the tiniest shrew scampers. The yawns of owls. The clicking of beaks. Even the slithering of snakes.

But these noises were symphonies compared to what came from the truck, or rather what was being done to the truck. These local yokels were taking it apart, piece by piece. Grating and wrenching the grill and its underlayment of hard rubber. The goofy guy used a crowbar from the back of the truck to wrench the tailgate off—my lovely twelve light tailgate!

He had a hard time with the screws and rivets, so he used a battery-powered metal saw to remove the hinges. Then the rattail, the crowbar. One big breath power-pull and it was off. Meanwhile the doofus with the spray can came around.

The pinon-scented, high desert air quickly turned foul with the odor of virulent VOCs. These are volatile organic compounds that have caused nose-pinching since they were invented. I remember hating spray paint in shop class in high school. But for me, now, as a dog person, these wind-driven solvents were a nose-nightmare of the very worst kind …

I had to close my burning eyes and bury my sensitive nose in my fluffy belly fur to keep myself from sneezing.

And then, of course, I sneezed!

The night stopped. The machinations of the crickets blinked out. The wind lay low. The creeping men came after my sneeze. Fortunately, they were off by a long shot, and I took off. White-tailed hares sprinted every which way, out of my way. A coyote yipped in my face when I startled him up from his torn meal of dead, slack bullsnake.

I kept running …

…until I realized I didn't have to.

Chapter Thirteen

How sweet it is when you figure it out.

Or as Roger Z. once said, "One night out does not give a novice werewolf a graduate degree in woodlore."

Make that a weredog, in my case.

Suffice to say, I almost ran into an owl that had just landed on a woodrat.

The truck wreckers were on my tail, too, coming down the arroyo full speed in low-low, churning sand and singing Dixie for the hell of it. Also shooting a high-powered rifle which was sending lead zinging into the sand.

The owl was raising claws to my face when I took the dare of a lifetime and trembled myself into its wide open, goldeneyed face.

And then, in a hoot-and-a-half, we were airborne. Not the two of us, the one of us. For I was it and it was I. I felt the wind in my face, and dog that I was I craved to bark at the pure joy of being bird. What came out was a cross between a hoot and woof.

I soared over the mudders in my old truck. Flight was effortless, it seemed. One whack of the wings and you were jetting north. I trembled still, however, to know the direction I was taking. But now, even riding the dark tide of night, I could see afar. The sleeping Sangres were mountain dreaming up ahead. Below I saw the town of Madrid, a ghost town again in swaths of moon gauze, and its myriad old time tinny roofs and flat roofs, and then we were beyond Madrid and owling north, ever north.

Soon we could see the slumbering sparks of Santa Fe and the smoke of many chimneys. I trembled toward home, The Veranda, northeast of town. And the stolen wings took me there. I landed awkwardly in a dead cedar only a matter of feet from our apartment. The lights were still on in our chamber roost on the second floor. So Laura was still up. How long had I been gone? How many hours? Was dawn about to stain the sky red?

Suddenly there was no time to wonder. A gaggle of ravens hit me from all sides. This was their tree, I supposed, and I was in for a clashing of claws and beaks. Ravens and crows loathe owls, their mortal enemies. But I, in good standing in the moment, was a kind of immortal, and I showed them what owl claws could do in the dark. They fended with battering wings, and a beak or two cut into my parry and thrust. But I had the upper hand... wing, I mean, and took them by surprise with round skull head butts, which they hadn't counted on. Two went fluttering off like black puffs of smoke.

There were two or three left. I screeched to scare them. That worked for a second or two. Gave me enough time to drop to the ground and tremble free of my owlishness. Momentarily, I was ... nothing.

Had I used up my tremble time?

Nothing fears nothing.

I ran and left the dazed, but still brazen, owl to fend for itself.

Running, I found myself phosphorescent.

I had no body to speak of, but I did have mind.

"Al-lan," I called.

He answered. "I am the thing you call phosphorescence. Bodiless. Formless. The air of night transfused into particle light drenched in moisture."

I felt a moment of great panic overcome me.

"How do I get back into my human form?"

"Tremble into me," he replied, "and I will deposit you into me, or rather you."

He did that thing so quickly I had no need of worry or fear.

The next thing I knew I was me. Hands, legs, head, and all.

"Where are you, Al-lan? I asked.

"Did you forget how I presented myself?"

Dog, I told myself.

And there he was again, the beautiful black dog I had been only a short time before. "I must go," he said. Then added with a chuckle, "Your wife Laura is waiting for you."

"It must be almost morning," I said.

He laugh-woofed.

"Your wife will tell you the time. Meanwhile, tell me quickly, my friendly shifter, how did it go with the Mudder Truckers."

"Is that the name of their gang?"

"They call themselves that, yes. Did you see your truck?"

"What is left of it."

"I was afraid of that. I must go now."

And with that, he plunged off into the phosphorescent night.

I returned, heavy-footed and human, to our little apartment.

"Where were you, Mr. Trembleman?" she said, as I entered through the front door.

I was about to tell her when she said, "So I talked to our detective. He saw the truck down in Cerrillos. Says the thief, or thieves, are selling pieces of it, here and there, but mostly at Capital Scrap. He's planning to make an arrest there in the morning."

"Could you tell me how long was I gone?"

She made a face. "Five minutes. Why?"

"I seem to have misplaced myself."

She smiled. "You always do that when you tremble. Maybe you should give that a rest for a while."

I felt tiny little prickles at the back of my neck.

"I was gone five minutes?"

"Not a minute more."

Chapter Fourteen

We went to bed sometime thereafter. But not before Laura told me that she thought the insurance company might not cover the replacement value of the truck. I thought of the guys I'd seen through canine eyes. "Mudders," I mumbled to Laura, who was already half asleep. "Mudder fokkers," but by then she was asleep and didn't hear my clever moniker for the truck crooks.

We slept soundly, or at least she did. I had troubled dreams. Fanatical coyotes with razor sharp fangs, dogs speaking the King's English, mist permutations, owl perturbations. I dreamed of Al-lan's face, yet he had no face. In the dream he was a darkness-faced nothingness with a voice of a growly dog. But that wasn't the way he was at all, and somehow I knew this even when dreaming.

I dreamed a baby in a birdcage. And then I was waiting in Walmart while a man in front of me paid the cashier one hundred dollars in dollar bills, counting them out endlessly. I looked behind me and there was a glitzy green leprechaun wearing a shamrock cape. He had a tall green top hat and he was black of face. Then I saw the messy killing of a fat possum. Murdered by a murder of crows, "All guts and no glory" I heard one of them say.

Mick showed up in the dream. He said, "Teresina's dead."

I woke up hearing that gravelly Mick voice in my ears. Soft Texas hardnail wind off the Brazos. So sure, so sad, so definitive.

Then, lying in bed, listening to my heart skip beats, I heard the real nightmare.

It was coming through the walls, as if piped by a supermarket stereo system.

Loud and clear.

Ooh and ah and umph.

A progression of bedspring banging.

Piglike grunts, squeals, nasty night noises of exertion such as I've never heard, and believe me, I've heard some. But these took the cake.

Then ... a spell of dead quiet.

Followed by some one, or some thing, licking the walls.

Giving new meaning to the expression, "speaking in tongues."

The slurping continued. I lay there, and listened.

I had a funny taste in my mouth. As if I had been eating garbage. Scarfing McD's pancakes off the street. Eating down owl-kills. There was a back blow of sickness, a succession of evil, that seeped through me. I woke Laura because I couldn't take being alone with the tonguing, the slap lather of wet tongue against cold midnight adobe.

"You hear?" I said, "I've been listening to that for about a half hour."

"They say he lifts weights," she murmured so sleepily I knew she wasn't really awake yet.

She was struggling to get there, swimming up out of that deep sea of distant swells and dreams.

"I lift weights," I said to her, "But I never make noises like that. I've never heard noises like that. This is insane."

She was yawning, blinking into wakefulness.

Once conscious, Laura is more wakeful than most, and she said: "You do know that Gabriela and Jeff downstairs moved out of their former apartment because they were right underneath all of that outpouring of nasty affection or whatever it is. I prefer to think heavy weights in the hands of a small fat Frog King named Appleplum."

"And ... if the King is fucking his own princess?"

"Since you put it so sweetly, then we get out, go somewhere else."

Some moments later, there were sirens.

We got out of bed, dressed, and went out on our balcony.

"I didn't know there were that many police cars and EMTs and ambulances and ..."

"I'm going downstairs," I said. "You'll be able to see it better down in the parking lot. You coming?"

"I've had enough excitement for one night," she said. "I'll make some coffee. I doubt we'll go back to sleep."

Down below, around the north side of our building I counted no less than ten emergency vehicles. It was like a mobile, flashing light hospital had cornered the parking lot.

Oddly, I saw no observers, which made it all the more dreamlike. Then, to add more mystery to it, there were no cops anywhere. No EMTs. One policeman seemed to be reporting down the hill because I could hear his radio making the usual hoarse coming and going chipping noises, as he spoke with someone at headquarters. My eyes roved but could see nothing except the afterburn of orange glare. The whole night was crisscrossed with rainbow beams of staccato color. I walked downhill. The number of vehicles increased astronomically as I descended to the Dumpster where the last cop car was parked at an angle so that no one could escape.

Was this a grand robbery? Maybe one of the largest heists ever seen in Santa Fe? Or ever not seen?

I waited in the chill early spring air. The Sangres had a little snowcap. The lower mountains were smoky in the faded moon. I heard wing flaps; the ravens were up. I wondered what the animals thought of this human circus. Then I knew. There was an enveloping symphony of coyote cries. All joined, as if on call, so to say. One great piercing, interwoven coyote shout!

I looked over my shoulder and suddenly there was Mick. His hoodie up high over his head, his eyes grey in the fractured light. About all I could really see of him was his eyes. He was raincoated and caped, hidden. But I could see his granite eyes were wet. Tears running down his shadowed cheeks.

"Teresina," I said. It just came out of my mouth.

He nodded, jerked his hoodie tighter. "Going back up now. She needs me."

"Is she alive?"

Saying no more, Mick turned and walked into the pulsating swords of red and blue light. Behind him, in the cemetery, dueling junipers winnowed the dark air and a raven rasped a sawblade of mistrust in human affairs. The night drew a short breath, as if it too was guilty of an unspoken crime of the heart.

Chapter Fifteen

Gabriela was in our apartment when I returned.

Her face was flushed and she was in full make-up. Candy apple red lipstick and very black eyeliner. She wore a loose flowery tunic, black leggings, flats. As usual she appeared to be in a play, but one of her own choosing. She was quite a woman.

I felt drained. I needed no more theater at that moment. But there is no denying Gabriela. She was one of the most undeniable people on the planet. She shot from the hip and seldom—no, never—missed.

"Were you there?" I asked.

"Just after." Her eyes widened. I wondered, could this incident at Mick's slow Gabriela down a little? But she went on, full steam. "I saw her, Teresina. All crumpled and worn, used up and still lovely but dying as I stood there, I could feel her taking last breaths, but she's still alive, right? I've seen lots of people dying, I've had them die in my arms, after all I was an emergency room nurse for twenty years as I think you know, and seeing Teresina like that was par for the course, but then, she's somebody you know pretty well, not just a drop in drop dead person, sorry to say it that way, and I had this creepy, crrreeeepy, feeling, you know, that maybe the Frog King as we call him had something to do with this, I mean, the Filipino couple went absolutely gorilla bonkers just before the cops and the EMTs showed up and did you hear the coyotes howl, one great big blast, just one not two, and then they shut up, and you could hear the cottonwoods growing."

She stopped talking. I started to say something, "Well, I was out there in the parking lot, and—"

"—Did you see Mick?" She cut in.

"He was kind of all over the place not knowing what to do with himself, and just being in the way, but the poor thing didn't know what else to do, so he was everywhere at the same time and I figured none of us needed to be there, really, except the cops thought we were immediate family and I guess in a way we are being so close-living here, you know. Anyway I left right after seeing her. She was ghosting."

"Ghosting … does that mean what I think it means?" Laura asked.

There was a faint rap on the door and Jeff was there. His eyes did not have their usual bright miming light of wide blue, and he sat quickly on the corner of the couch and rested his chin on his palm.

"Ghosting means," Gabriela continued, "going away from the body and leaving the old shell behind. There wasn't much left of her there that I could see."

"Jeff, were you there, too?" I asked.

He shook his head. I looked sideways at him and he looked like he was in a different play from Gabriela. He was a collapsed wooden soldier, his mustache still strong and uplifted, his chin square and rugged, but the rest of him looked sad and broken. Laura offered herbal tea and they accepted.

For an unusual while we all sipped ginger, spirit lifting tea, in silence.

"I got more information on ye olde Frog King," Gabriela said. "His life seems to have started in 1995. Before then, there's nothing, and believe me, I looked everywhere on the internet. He didn't exist before then … did I already tell you that? She, Tutu—"

"—Sometimes we call her Miss Piggy," Jeff interjected, chuckling.

"We call her Petunia sometimes," Laura remarked, "but Tuto's her stage name and when she gets on her dancing outfit, and goes down the path with her disproportionately large—"

"Ass!" Gabriela snapped. "Sorry to butt in."

We all laughed.

"Well, she does have one," Gabriela went on, "and all the more visible when she wears leotards, I mean let's be honest, the woman's a beer barrel, her arms are like hawsers, and she got that odd, little flattened pig face, I swear they're all from another planet, don't you think, Jeff?"

Jeff, sleepy-eyed, snapped to, and said, "Pluto, most likely." For a moment his face was fully animated. Then, "I think we'd better call it a night, folks. I'm really bushed."

They left, promising to keep us posted on Teresina's "progress."

We smoked a little herb to quiet our nerves.

In a matter of minutes there was a forceful knock on the door.

Gabriela's raps were always soft, so this wasn't she, and it turned out to be two brown uniformed officers of the law. Sheriff's deputies, I figured.

They came in abruptly, both seemingly nervous at the invasion. "We're checking the apartments to find out if anyone knows anything more about what happened in 1805 tonight. Sorry for the intrusion. People will forget or overlook something if we don't ask right away." This from a man who had his right hand resting comfortably on his pistol handle.

"Someone said there was a shriek over here and we wanted to check it out," the second deputy said, scratching his chin.

Laura and I both laughed.

"What's funny about that?" the pistol cop said.

"Well," I said seriously, "you see that's George over there. He's been with us for over 40 years and, well, sometimes he lets out a loud yell when there's a lot of emotion or disturbance in the air."

"Let's have a word with George," the partner said.

I went across the room and uncovered George's cage, revealing a big, bright green, gold and blue Amazonian parrot. As if to table the discussion, George let out an ear shattering squawk.

"Does he do that often?" the first deputy asked.

"Just when there's uniformed visitors in the middle of the night," Laura said.

"We're not visitors," the second man said. "We're officers of the law."

"We can see that," I mentioned. "But you haven't introduced yourselves yet … George doesn't know who you are …"

"Neither do we," Laura said.

"Let me see your identification," the first officer said with a sigh, "and we'll trouble you no more."

"You know," I said, "the Santa Fe Police couldn't get any identification from the guy who lives next door. They interviewed him and came out of there as baffled as we've been for the past few months. The man has no ID. What I'm saying, there's something unusual going on in that apartment, and you should be over there interviewing them, not us, but anyway here's my ID." I gave the first officer my driver's license. He squinted at it, passed it back to me with a grim nod.

George, who'd been watching with his head cocked, suddenly burst out laughing. He has a funny barroom laugh, sort of a guttural mafioso thing, but only when something strikes him funny. Apparently this did.

The gun-gripping officer shuddered and looked around, as if the walls had produced that sound. His partner flinched and made a face. Then they looked at each other, shrugged, and shook their heads. It embarrasses people when they're afraid of George.

Once, a cameraman doing a shoot for a magazine, got a little too close to George. George attacked, open clawed, and cut the man's forehead. This was just after he'd bragged about filming Bengal tigers, saying he wasn't afraid of a little parrot (actually George is quite large and can get mad for no reason but usually it's offensive male egos that set him off).

However, this time, George was in his cage. But I could tell he didn't like the way these men looked. He didn't like their uniforms or their presentation. Or lack of same.

A moment later, they were clumping out the door.

From inside the apartment we heard them walk across the landing in their heavy boots. The gun guy said, "Who in their right mind would keep an animal like that?"

"It's not an animal, it's a bird," his partner said.

"Same difference."

We heard two palpable knocks on the Frog King's door.

Chapter Sixteen

There was terrible arguing for ten minutes. After which, the deflated deputies emerged, heads down.

I stuck my head out of the door. "What happened?"

They turned at the stairwell, descended without a word.

I watched them walk down the sidewalk to the parking lot. Their footfalls echoing in the elm-rustling night.

From their straight-backed walk, and their silence, I knew.

Somehow, Frog King Appleplum had exerted his mesmeric influence upon these two flat-footed, starched up cops. And now they were wilted.

I heard maniacal laughter in the King's castle.

Then zombie silence. And then …

… the predictable, horrible, usual squealing and moaning. Unearthly exhortations of sexual deviltry.

The Girl was having orgasms again and Frog King was wantonly administering his personal needle of love.

Sometimes I tried not to imagine what Tutu Petunia was doing with The Boy. But the imagination—on hearing unknown and unmentionable sounds—will go places the heart doesn't want to follow. Then, hearing more and more unmentionables, the heart goes reluctantly, and sees things even the mind can't imagine. This was one of those times.

But it all came to an abrupt end.

Suddenly the merry-go-round of illicit love came to a stop. The Girl threw open the door and ran out naked into the night. Laura and I witnessed the streaming of her long black hair and the svelte body gleam in soft moonstream.

Her scream so loud it tore the veil of Veranda secrecy.

Who could sleep after that?

It chilled the blood. As much as the image of the naked girl enflamed the imagination: her hair rivering down her back as she ran away from the horror. Of what, we could only imagine. But there was blood in it, we feared.

We put in a call to the campus police, the so-called Courtesy Police provided by The Veranda. The all-night reprievers of nightmares such as this.

"What is the nature of your call, please?" a soft neutral voice said almost in a whisper.

"I believe there's been a rape in 1804," I said. My voice quavered.

"Exactly what time do you think this happened?"

"Just around now. Please check the lower campus of The Veranda because there is a young girl, a teenager, running for her life."

"What condition is she in, sir?"

"She's naked."

"Very well, sir, we'll look into it."

"I bet you will!" Then: "What's wrong with you people? Did you not hear what I just said? There's a naked kid who's just been raped running for her life."

"Where exactly is she running, sir?"

"She's running away from Death."

"Going where, sir, and with whom?"

Laura grabbed the phone and shouted into the receiver.

"You are all a bunch of fucking idiots!"

She slammed the phone down.

Then she burst into tears.

I spent the rest of the night talking her down, getting up and going to the window, peeking out. Of course, the Courtesy Police never showed. We knew, as well, that unless there was a recording, Management would do nothing. After all, Management and CP were the same organization. What was a rape anyway? Not as bad as a murder, which was what Gabriela was saying happened to Teresina. Mick wasn't talking. Neither was Management. When we phoned the SF Police, we sometimes got Detective Archuleta who wanted only to talk about the retrieval of the F150. Murder aside, rape notwithstanding, there was a truck impounded, and one of the goofy guys in a jail cell, not talking.

Progress is a strange thing. It comes to the human scene, in fits and starts. It goes away. It comes back. It's loved and hated. It's not noticed.

***

The following morning after a sleepless night and a long conversation by cellphone regarding The Girl and Frog King, Children's Protective Services got interested in the case, AND PROMISED TO CALL BACK!

By afternoon the SFP were back at our door, this time to report a complaint. Someone living in an apartment below us had heard, and then seen, someone answering to my description, carrying a box with a screaming baby down to the parking lot. Fortunately, the cop who'd knocked at our door, was a native, a Pueblo Indian, and when he heard me say that I had taken our parrot George down to our newly acquired Subaru (gift of sister-in-law), he did something we would've done: he laughed.

Still, I had to go down the hill and face a contingent of fresh cops, who asked the following question:

"How do you know, it wasn't a baby? Someone here at The Veranda heard it."

The smiling American Indian cop said, "He already explained to me that it was his pet parrot. They make a lot of noises. Some of them scream like little babies. I've heard it at the Pueblo, my uncle has one."

"A screaming parrot?" the sergeant asked.

"Yes."

"Look." I said. We take George—that's our parrot—to have his nails trimmed at Feathered Friends. I ease the car ride for him by putting a blanket over his carrying-cage and sometimes the sudden transport scares him. He screamed once, that's all."

"This gentleman here," the sergeant said, "says there was a lot of wailing, little suffering baby sounds, coming from that box there." He pointed to the inside of the Subaru.

I glanced at the "gentleman", an overweight, thuggy-looking guy, unshaven and angry. He glared at me.

"My parrot speaks whole English sentences," I said in my best non-sequitur manner. Then I opened the back door of the car and lifted the blanket off George's traveling cage, so the five or more cops could see the bird.

George screamed.

***

The following day I got Allstate on the phone. Actually, it wasn't Allstate. It was, but it wasn't: it was Hester at Allstate, and she said, "We'll give you 1200.00 for your truck, and that's the best we can do considering the shape it's in."

I took a deep breath.

"The shape it's in is because three crooks stole the truck, a classic 1993 F150 by the way, and then took it mudding in some arroyo and beat hell out of it. Then, they salvaged the dashboard, the ignition, the steering wheel, almost the entire interior, but for the liner which they smothered with Valentine love notes—I am not kidding about this—and all of the exterior chrome parts, bumpers etc., tailgate and—"

"—Jack, sorry to interrupt … may I call you Jack?"

"Yes, that's my name."

"Okay, I see from our paperwork that your truck is, in fact, a classic model but our adjuster says you kept it pretty badly. It's in awful shape."

"I just explained that. They, the thieves who stole it from the parking lot of The Veranda, which has no security whatsoever, destroyed the truck. Look, I have a photograph taken a few months ago and it shows the shape the truck was in prior to the theft."

"Why didn't you say so?"

"I just did. Why weren't you listening?"

There was a moment of silence during which I heard papers being shuffled, and a muffled conversation. Then Hester came back and said, "I see from your file that you've been with us for, let's see now—"

"—Almost fifty years," I said.

"Wow! That's a really long time, Jack. Did you send the snapshot of the truck yet?"

"My wife is sending it as we speak."

She exclaimed, "Oh, wow! I see that you've been with us for … fifty years? And you've had no accidents? None? How's that even possible?"

"Good driving?"

She laughed. "OK, Jack. That said, let's talk about fair value. Your truck is …hmmm. Let's say, very good condition!"

"Did you get the photo my wife sent?"

Hester hummed. "OK, I see it now … oh, my, you're not kidding. This is beautiful!"

"Was …"

"And we're terribly sorry for your loss, but, hold on a minute, will you?"

Hester put me on hold, and I said to Laura, "We're getting somewhere, I think."

We waited until Hester came back. "Happy to say, Jack, we can offer you market value, in terms of the area, the region where the truck resides, or rather resided."

"So you're saying, if I sold it here in the condition it's in, was in, high value would be the classic market price in Santa Fe, New Mexico where these good old trucks are highly valued."

"You got it, Jack. We will issue that check tomorrow based on Kelly Blue Book."

For the first time in weeks, I felt like things were beginning to ravel rather than unravel.

We went forthwith to our favorite restaurant, La Choza, to celebrate. Got our names in at the hostess desk, and then went outside to wait the usual 30 minutes. We took a walk down by the railyard. There was a red caboose parked on the silver rails and on the side of it there was a plaque in honor of the donor. It said, "In Memory of Abe Silver Who Loved Santa Fe With All His Heart."

I smiled. I remembered Abe. That's the thing about Santa Fe. People don't disappear here, they live on in the memory of others. As will our lost, pummeled, beloved seven hurricane savior F150 truck.

A little later, we found ourselves at a table and our waiter, Juneau, was a good friend of cousin Shane, which made the green chile clam chowder taste all the better, and the rellenos and sopaipillas better still.

One margarita each, salt and bitter and sweet all at the same time. The rime on the glass, the lime in the glass.

Laura and I had ordered our dessert when we first sat down. That was in honor of our friend Roger Zelazny who had a general fear that there might be a run on the desert item he wanted; so he put in his dessert order first, just like a little kid. We ordered the signature mocha cake in his honor.

Thus we were able to set aside the stolen truck, which, incidentally, had already appeared in Trent Zelazny's novel, *Wrong World*.

I liked to think of it as *Right Truck, Wrong World*.

Chapter Seventeen

Call it tornadic memory, if you will.

We were having quite a whirly spell of memory, where, surprisingly, everything meets up in the middle. Where everything, every strand of personal history, is woven together. A lady named Tony follows us out of Albertson's supermarket and says she remembers us, as well we remember her. "How long has it been?" she asks. "Your daughters were something like three and eight."

Laura said, "We knew you forty years ago."

Later, on our way to get our hair cut at Yvonne's Salon, I mentioned the poem I wrote back then in those good old golden hours of youth. Laura remembered, as I recited the four tight love lines—

> We sat listening,
> Penitents ourselves.
> Holding hands, in love.
> In canyon time.

That was fifty years ago. We were in the Gallinas Canyon sitting together on a first date. We were in a high dry, water flume way up on the canyon rim.

First there were coyotes, then the plaintive, distant song of the Penitentes, so Moorish in resonance. The shadow of the canyon deepening as we looked and listened, holding hands.

I touched Laura's face and there were tears coming down her cheeks, and she said, "It's so beautiful." I knew we would always be together then, for she and I could cry at beauty seen and beauty felt.

And now, all these years later, children grown to women with children of their own. We were grandparents, still hand holding, still loving in the canyon lands.

The hair salon was in the Southside house of Yvonne. As we came in the door her pit bull grabbed hold of my left hand. Then it led me, rather strongly, into the salon.

I felt the pressure on my hand, but instead of resisting, I gave the dog more of me, so that instead of biting down harder, it spit my hand out. A trick I'd learned long ago from martial arts teacher, Kelvin Rodriquez, who used to say, "Always give them more than they can chew."

Soon Yvonne was snipping away. "I drive that turquoise motorcycle out there on the porch," she said. "I hope my dog didn't hurt you. Look, see, I have some new bite marks from that one. He's a little rough with his teeth. I had a heart attack not too long ago. Not from the dog, probably from my rich diet. Anyways, I survived. That's all we can do, like my dad always says."

There was something trembler-like about Yvonne's touch. I asked her if she had ever studied the internal martial arts.

"I got a degree in massage, if that's what you mean."

"More than that," I said, "you have more than that in your hands. I can feel it."

"Maybe I got some special training from Alonzo. Do you remember him?"

"Alonzo Serrano?" Laura asked. "He was a blind curandero. We went to college with him. He gave special treatments to all of the runners at Santa Fe Preparatory in the 1980s."

I added, "He enabled me, at age forty, to teach my class in Sokol, which is a Czech martial art. Every time I threw my back out, Alonzo put it back in."

We all laughed. Then Yvonne said, "Well, that 'special treatment' you mention. He would ease the pain in my shoulders but his hands always slipped down to my breasts. I'd have to remind him: those don't hurt me, just my shoulder, OK? That man was something else. He loved breasts."

"He told me one time," I said, "that he was the one who blew up the chem lab at Highlands U. So I asked him how he did that, and he told me, 'I don't know, I am blind.' So I told him that his hands could see very well indeed, and he told me, 'I have been a hand trembler almost since birth. My mother was one of those, too.'"

"Well, that was Alonzo, a very gifted man. But you had to watch his hands slipping into places they didn't belong."

"Blind man's bluff," I remarked.

Laura laughed. Yvonne smiled.

She said, "Alonzo called me Dances With Scissors. I called him Tickles with Disrespect. Well, he's gone now. My mother liked him."

"Where did he go?" I asked.

"Where we all go," she said.

Chapter Eighteen

For an hour I lost myself in the spiral convolution of a land snail that had crawled up our slider door. I marked my meditation time by the snail's invisible progress and said to myself, "Welcome to the world of all things great and snail …"

I wondered if Al-lan could fit into a carapace so small.

What would it feel like if he could?

Like nothing?

Like his dog's garb or like my flying owl fortress?

Thinking about this took me back to the very first time I trembled on the farm.

I was five years old.

And I was alone looking at a pattern of light coming in through the cedarshutters of our mountaintop house. My mother was in the kitchen. I felt the opening of the kitchen door, and across the floor some dust mice scattered. I followed one of them into an open closet door in the living room. The darkness beckoned me. I went in.

And closed the door to the degree that only a thin blade of light cut into the sanctuary of silence, dark, dustmouse secrecy.

Now, what? I asked myself.

And then it happened …

My left arm tickled, but when I itched it, it tickled more.

This went on for some time. I shook my arm and felt an explosion of energy in my left hand. It seemed that light came out of it—pincers of gold. I could move these pincers with my mind. I could clip the hanging raincoats that hung above me, and shake them.

I closed my eyes and saw the creek at the bottom of the hill. I used the golden pincers to latch on to a sunken log one branch of which was sticking out of the water like a gnarled hand.

The branch hand and my hand met. I was in the water then but I didn't feel cold. I was one with it, like some kind of newt or salamander.

I moved about luxuriantly in the bubbling creek bottom.

I saw a turtle and touched his face. He didn't seem to see, or feel, my touch.

I came out of the cold creek and stood in the sunshine.

I saw a snail on a stone.

At that same moment, my mother found me in the closet.

I had closed the door and was in complete darkness.

She was surprised to find me all alone in the dark.

She couldn't see my trembling left arm and hand.

Nor could she see the golden pincers that allowed me to go to realms beyond my sight.

***

For years I have held this vision in my head and heart.

Whenever life became too much for me as a kid I retreated into a closet and used the tremble and the pincers to disappear into another world.

It was more than an escape; it was a spiritual awakening that I was unable to share with anyone. It was just between me, myself and I, as we used to say.

And now, as an older person, some seventy years later, I remember seeing that snail so long, long ago.

The beauty of the creature that carried its house on its back. A creature with horns. Sightless but fully equipped with vision.

As an adult in my twenties I had lost the art of trembling, given it up, almost forgotten it entirely when, by some miracle, Laura and I were lost on the coast highway in northern, California, and I trembled.

The direction shown, I knocked on the door of a dark house. A man came to the door and I begged to know where we might find some kind of hostel.

"The fog stopped us," I said. "Otherwise we would've kept going."

"Come in," the man said.

My hand trembled as we entered his house, as if I'd been there before.

It turned out, he was a roshi, a tai chi master, and, quite miraculously, the former husband of a nextdoor neighbor in the town where I grew up 3,000 miles away on the opposite coast. Such things happen. Does trembling make them happen?

So there we were, lost in the mist of the Pacific cypress coast, and now someone had invited us into his warm, firelit home and was making potato soup for us.

Then while the potatoes were boiling, our host invited us into his backyard where a chiminea was glowing.

There, between the rolling waves on the nearby beach and the vast bands of incoming fog, this remarkable man did tai chi, calmly and gracefully, as if he were in a dream. After a little while he asked us to join him.

We followed his fluid movements, one after another, doing our best to follow his flow.

I remember looking down at my feet and there were vast trails of snails, leaving tracks of silvery night-slime. The fog enveloped us. The Master moved with the snails, never so much as touching them. We followed him. In the salt crystal, black coastal night air, I somehow remembered the closet and the creek. My left arm tingled and the mild electricity traveled down the bone-line to my fingertips. And then beyond. I felt the golden pincers extend and I could reach out and gently brush aside some of the snails and make a delicate, narrow path between them. Of course, the Master needed no path; he flowed like fog and grazed no shell.

But there we were at land's end in Monterey. Once lost, now found.

Not far from the myths of Tortilla Flat.

On a foggy, foggy snail walk.

Somewhere between Sweet Thursday and Cannery Row.

Chapter Nineteen

And now I was listening to wind and sirens, trailers and trucks. The fast moving, discordant sounds of St Francis Drive.

It was early morning in Santa Fe. To the east the sun was buttering the graveyard on the other side of the coyote fence. Spring warblers were singing, far off crows were cawing. Tight green buds on the cottonwoods. Juniper berries hard emerald. Aspens, gray-barked and budless.

I was in a zone, as they say, when, behind me on the stairs the family of miscreants appeared, one after another.

I was sure they wouldn't speak—in three months they hadn't said a word to us, except for The Boy whom we overheard once, as he came up the sidewalk.

But I was wrong.

The man spoke very clearly in a sort of unreal radio voice from the 1930s.

"My name is Tony Appleplum," he said in his stentorian style.

I was so stunned that I missed his wife's name. She seemed to understand this and said in a nasal tone, "My name's Fiona, pleased to meetya."

The Girl was there, too, but you couldn't see her face. The glossy curtain of straight hair fell across the front of her body to her waist. She stepped around me quickly and disappeared down the stairs.

Her brother, if that's what he was, had a mechanical brightness in his eyes. He was holding a small terrier-type dog. The moment I looked at it, the animal sailed out of The Boy's arms and bit my knee.

Tony Appleplum noticed this and grinned. So did Fiona. Then Tony saluted me, as if we were soldiers in the same campaign. For a moment, I saw them exactly as they were—almost all the same height, even the gone girl named The Girl.

They were all short and blocky and had pushed-in faces with flattened lips and grey eyes, each one of them. The eyes seemed battery-operated, and they moved queerly in their eye sockets.

The Girl was the exception ... or was she? I'd never seen her face really, just dark facets of her body in a candlelit room. Had I imagined that she was pretty? Was this nothing more than my fantasy?

For this collective family was anything but pretty. In the hard light of day, they were the living dead, somnolent white zombies in a low budget film series.

"We're off to meet Big Yellow," Appleplum said.

"Big Yellow?"

I was rubbing my knee where the dog had torn my jeans and wounded me.

The little beast was still growling. The Boy was holding him, or her, and had the same face as the mutt only minus the fur.

"It's a school bus," The Boy said smartly. "A long tubular, yellow and black amalgamation of metal, rubber, paint, and mirror with, of course, one unusually nasty bus driver."

I nodded. The Boy's face was so well-flattened it looked like that same school bus had run over it twice.

Tony Appleplum saluted sharply once more and I gave them extra room on the stairs and they tromped off. At the sidewalk, Tony Appleplum had a tiny bicycle waiting for him. "Now file in behind me, son," he ordered The Boy.

I could not even say Fiona. The bulgy tutu woman was Petunia.

"You go, girl," he said to her and obediently she took to the sidewalk doing a funny little dance step she'd learned in trimnastics class. She was tightly packed into her tutu. Her black leotards looked painted on. From a rearview angle, her bulbous butt looked like a granite boulder on Sun Mountain.

I went upstairs to put Neosporin ointment on the knee.

Laura listened to my improbable meeting, which I called "The Affair on the Stair."

When I'd revealed every detail, she shook her head, said, "Last night—did you hear them? —for some reason I couldn't sleep. There was this bubbling current of high pitched voices which I would swear were not human."

"What'd they sound like?"

"Dolphins, whales. Abysmal grunts. Ultrasonic squeals. Weird isn't the word for it. Extraterrestrial is."

That night I was awakened, not by the aliens, but by the tribe of singing mice in our kitchen. Gabriela told me they had the run of the whole complex. Every apartment, she said, had a family of mice. Under every sink there was a tunnel, an "interwoven mouse expressway," was what she called it.

I went into the kitchen and frightened them away.

Then I bent down, listened.

I could hear them singing far off in the labyrinths of the lost.

Not just singing.

Harmonically singing.

A veritable glee club of rodentia.

But, really, this was no laughing matter.

"Mice'll kill you," Gabriela had said. "They'll quietly and secretly gnaw off the epidermal layer of your skin. Honestly, as an Emergency Nurse I've seen what they can do to unprotected human feet—gnawed them to the quick—and as you know the fleas in their fur carry the plague."

Chapter Twenty

Bluejay showed up the following day.

His front teeth were missing and I asked him about that.

"My horse kicked them out," he said, and said no more.

But even without those front teeth he did a beautiful blessing in our kitchen. It was from The Blessing Way Chant where all is blessed above and below and all around.

He sang of the dwellings of the deities and the places where they dwelt.

> House made of dawn
> House made of moss
> House made of cotton
> House made of rain
> House made of sun
> House made of turquoise
> House made of wind
> House made of fur
> House made of pollen
> House made of flint
> House made of crystal

At the end our hands were joined and he spoke the final blessing.

"Deities of all houses under heavens, bless this house made of mud, resin and pine. Bless this family made of blood, marrow and bone."

To me, he whispered, "I should have pollen from the cornflower to sprinkle in the four directions, and above and below, this will make our days longer."

A little time passed and he said nothing. Then he nodded and said very softly, "We must keep going, you and I. Keep telling our stories. We have far to go. We need to leave our mark on the cliffside." He laughed. Then, "The Hero Twins were not really twins, you know. Those two: Nayenezgani and

Tobachischin. The first born is Born-Of-Sunlight. The second son is Born-Of-Water. You know them as such?"

I said that I did. "They are brothers. The ones who ridded the Navajolands of monsters brought about by the misconduct of women."

"Do you know what they did?"

I smiled. "I've read about it at The Wheelright Museum. They masturbated with cholla cactus. I've always marveled at their tolerance for pain or their love of masochistic self-sex."

Jay didn't smile. "They cut off the thorns and used the arm of the cholla which, as you know, is slick with cactus juice."

"Now I get it. Even mythologically, it was confusing."

I gave Jay a cup of Navajo tea that Laura had brewed.

"I guess it's good," Jay said with a measure of suspicion. "Where did it come from?"

"From a friend at Pine Springs Elementary School," Laura said, as she placed some strudel on the table.

We sipped and chewed.

"Those brothers were gods," Jay said, "but it didn't keep them from getting into trouble. One thing to remember—they were brothers, not twins. Calling them Hero Twins as many non-tribal interpreters have done is wrong."

"So, you're saying that many of these old stories get messed up in the retelling. Like you said to me one time, Spider Woman isn't really a spider. She doesn't have eight legs."

"That's right," Jay confirmed. "She was just a woman who wove like a spider. Her fingers, the old ones say, moved fast. Just like a spider weaving a rain-jeweled web."

Jay removed his battered grey cowboy hat. "Let me take my ego off for a moment," he said with a grin.

I noticed that his hair was "nuthatched" like mine.

That is to say, dusted grey.

The story goes, the dust came off Nuthatch, that little greyish bird, as Nuthatch flew over the heads of The People. This gave them a good dusting.

Then Gopher gave them toothache, Coyote stole Water Monster's babies and brought on the great flood. He also stole the stars, but that is another story.

Sometimes I wonder about these things. The ancient Navajo stories remind me of Genesis. So do the sacred tales of other cultures.

According to certain Kabbalists, it wasn't a serpent that offered Eve the apple, it was a camel.

Well, there has to be a coyote or a Jackal in there somewhere.

But if not, a camel will have to do.

There is a so-called thirteenth moon in the Navajo calendar. The People call it a Coyote Moon.

The anthropologist in me might suggest that something along this order may have come from the ice steppes of Mongolia.

But, in any case, there were hogans under that ill-begotten moon.

And a wolf-hooded man with a trickster's grin and a great talent for telling tales, said, "Thirteen is one more than twelve."

He took a medicine bag full of stolen stars with him when he quit the campfire that night. And to show his pleasure, he raised his head and howled at his own named thirteenth moon.

Chapter Twenty-One

I was dreaming.

Sometimes I heard voices in my dreams and they dictated passages from books I would later write.

The voice this time said:

"If God gave dog to man to keep him from being lonely … and He gave cat to woman so she could see God, then Horse was God's gift to both so they could have, not holy matrimony, but rather holy mobility."

The voices sounded like N. Scott Momaday, the great Kiowa poet.

I was thinking about my dream when I heard a soft knock at the door.

It was Jay.

"I forgot to tell you something," he said from under the low brim of his cowboy hat. "Here," he added grinning, "a present."

He handed me a notebook-size painting in a sort of pastel brown and gray color.

"This is a painting I did of Spotted Pony, my father's horse."

It was the embodiment of my dream.

Jay said, "This goes with it. It's a portrait of my father on Spotted Pony. I did it from a photograph that was taken long ago."

I knew that these two works of art were sacred to him, and to me, as well, because I knew the significance, in Navajo lore, of the Father, as in Sun Father, and the power of the Sun Father's horse. That mythology had been told to me some forty years earlier. The horse with a sunbeam in his mouth for a bridle gave The People the power of mobility, just as the dream-speaker said.

I had heard stories of Jay's father, the medicine man, long before I met him in person and he blessed our house in Tesuque. I had known that he was a man of great power and that, given time, he would pass that power on to his son. Now I had the son, the father and the holy horse.

"I can't thank you enough for these portraits, Jay."

He smiled, nodded. "There is something else I want to give you. I was on the Jicarilla reservation," he explained, "and there's a lake there where they do the bear dance. I saw a flute lying by the shore. I wasn't sure whether it was made of wood or clay, so I picked it up and studied it for a good little while."

Jay removed his pale gray cowboy hat with the beaded band. He touched the creases with his fingers. His dark eyes surveyed our living room with its portraits of Sitting Bull, Geronimo and Bob Marley.

I noticed a small paper bag by his left leg. But he made no mention of it.

He continued with his story: "A blackbird then appeared at the lakeside. I knew then, at that moment, that this flute was not for me. That it was something holy … that it was something whose meaning I needed to better understand. Time passed and in that passage of time, I learned that the laws that govern men are an important part of the song the flute would make. This flute, I found out, belonged to a man named Kokopelli. Not the one you might know by this name. But a small worm with the same name. This little worm played the flute."

He waited before going on with his story.

"So … if you place a tiny pebble on the third hole of this flute, and you blow it into the stars something sacred will occur."

Jay paused, looked around the room again. Briefly his eyes traveled from Sitting Bull to Geronimo, then to Marley. I looked at these three great paintings, the eyes of the chiefs of the earth were on us, just as Jay's eyes were on them. For a nanosecond, Marley's serious eyes seemed to smile.

"You blow the pebble into the starway … into the cosmos. You make music of a different kind."

I asked him what would happen.

Jay said, "The pebble ensures that the laws that govern human beings will always be up there in the heavens."

I waited while he considered what to say, and how to say it.

At last he said, "The laws of Diné couldn't be written on stone or sand or even in a man's memory. In time, all those things wear away. The sacred laws

of governance had to be inscribed in the heavens forever. And so they remain."

After saying that, Bluejay put his hat on and said he had to go to the
Roundhouse to get the politicians to allocate money so the people in Crownpoint would have a renewable supply of water.

We walked out to his Jeep together. "It took a little round-backed worm
to blow that pebble to the stars," he said, laughing. Then he said softly, "I
want you to have the flute. Use it with care. It came from a long time back
and it has great power and can ensure harmony."

He gave me the small brown paper bag.

I accepted it with gratitude, for it was a great honor to have it. But I knew
not to make too much of a given thing. Certainly not in the presence of the
giver.

I asked him then if he knew of the trouble we'd been having in the apartment complex.

He nodded. "I know of it."

I didn't need to ask how he knew.

He knew.

Before he left Santa Fe, he phoned me. "We got the water," he said. Then
he confided, "You don't need to blow a pebble to the stars, that is for a medicine man. All you need to do is paint some stars on a small round pebble. Put
it on the banco at the top of the stairs to the right of your door. If someone
steals it, paint another one just like it, and put that in the same place."

I said I would do what he said.

Chapter Twenty-Two

I painted the pebble as Jay described—four black stars in the ancient form of small black crosses hanging over a bent pine.

The pine tree could also have been a girl; a girl with her long straight hair caught in a blue stream of wind.

I placed it on the banco at the top of the stairs. One slight brush of the hand could've sent it flying over the edge and down to the valley of river rocks at the bottom of the stairs.

I had done my work. Now we'd wait and see how Jay's magic worked. Or did not.

That afternoon Laura made chile rellenos and put them between slices of fresh baked bread. We ate them on the balcony in the sun wind facing Rosario cemetery. Gabriela said, that same day, "The spirits from that place come in and out of these haunted apartments. I smell their cigarette smoke sometimes. A couple of times I've caught a skinny man dipping himself into the bathtub with me. I kicked him out."

"How did you do that?" Laura asked. She liked to hear Gabriela's explanation of confounding things like this.

Gabriela said, "With my foot." Her green eyes blazed like emeralds. "I wasn't about to play deadman's bluff with a real ghost," she went on. "Afterwards, that skinny guy still lingered, watching me as I got dressed. I let him have a good look at me, if that's what he wanted. Then I placed a leaf of life plant in a glass of spring water from Las Golondrinas. After which I lit a spliff of Cuban ganja and blew smoke in the four directions. Bingo, ghostie went away! Maybe you've seen him up in your apartment?"

I told her, "Sometimes I've noticed bitter, dirty sweat—"

"—graveyard ghost-sweat," Gabriela cut in.

"Someone, or something, makes coffee around 3:45 AM—"

"—That's him," Gabriela exclaimed. "That must be the hour he died."

"Did you know this person?" Laura asked.

"I do now," Gabriela replied.

"How can a spirit make coffee?" I asked.

She looked at me critically, then indulgently.

"He makes coffee just as you do. But—let me guess, he forgets the most important part of the procedure …"

Neither Laura, nor I, knew what she meant by that. Gabriela shook her head and let out a loud guffaw. "The coffee! When he makes coffee in our apartment, he forgets and leaves the coffee part out, so you just get boiled water."

Gabriela rubbed her eyes. "God knows all the things I've seen as a card-carrying psychic and being Cuban all these things aren't the least bit strange to me. What about you? The supernatural seems quite normal to me."

The conversation with Gabriela came back to me while we sat on the balcony having our sandwiches. No doubt, I thought, there's so much going on here in these ghost-ridden apartments. I cleansed my mind of it for a moment while looking at the snow on the Sangres beyond the cemetery. The spring wind was playing in the conifers. The high mountain snowmelt was sparking in the pungent, pine-sharp air. Red-winged warblers sang in a single, high-branched ponderosa. Ravens made their seesawing passes through the still barren, naked looking cottonwoods.

Across from where we sat we looked down on the new green grass of the cemetery and there was a Pueblo woman in a long raincoat standing in full sunshine. Her head was unbowed and she spoke, more or less casually, into a freshly dug grave.

She stayed and prayed, as we watched. The wind tickled her raincoat, lifting the bottom edges.

"Don't you wish we could hear what she says?" Laura said.

I nodded. "What's odd here, for me, is the living and the dead. You see and hear the living …"

"And you sometimes actually see the dead," Laura mentioned. "There seems to be no line between."

Later on, that same day, we learned that my favorite student from the early 90s died in Trinidad, Colorado. Crushed—he and his wife—by a woman who ran a red light. Both dead. The driver, alive and well. Or at least, alive.

This is what makes life and death so strange here in New Mexico, the sudden disappearance of someone you love. Dan and Lon gone so young. Will I see them again? Think so. Believe so. Know so.

But when?

The driver who killed them—what of her?

All we knew from what we heard was that she was just fine in her own skin. No injuries.

What to make of this?

Laura and I were both in shock.

***

That night, or rather early morning, at 3:45, I heard the coffee water perking and went into the kitchen to confront the ghost.

As I stood in the empty kitchen, a cupboard flew open.

Then there was a loud bang, like a gunshot.

I jumped and beans went flying all over the room, striking me in the head and chest.

Yes, BEANS! Bush's Baked Beans. A can of them had exploded.

By then, Laura was there with me and almost right away we stooped to the task of cleaning up.

"Nothing like cleaning up gaseous, stinking, rotten beans!" Laura said, cursing under her breath.

We got some old kitchen towels and rags under the sink, and began wiping walls, floors and cabinets. We used baking soda, vinegar, and aromatic cleansers of the commercial kind, and still the stink was omnipresent.

At sunrise we were caked in brown awfulness, but the kitchen was clean. We made some coffee, quaffed it, and took showers. As we toweled off, I said to Laura, "That's some afterlife, huh?"

"He'll be back," she said mildly, shaking her head. "That's the way he was. Always joking. He liked practical jokes more than anyone I ever knew."

"This was one hell of an impractical joke," I commented. "But you're right, it was a heap of Dan."

The day proved neither mystical nor dull, until evening when a red-throated hummingbird with a blue face showed up on the balcony. A furious-hearted little fellow who came buzzing right at my face. Then he whirled over my head and briefly landed on my baseball cap. Then he zoomed off into the sunset.

***

That night I dreamed white lightning, green lightning, yellow lightning, black lightning.

I smelled the cedar vapor.

I heard the night-dark hills speaking in low, rhythmic tones like Jay DeGroat.

I saw diamonds of dust on the Sun Father's great horse, Nightway.

I saw Monster Slayer, Nayenezgani, in flint armor, flashes of lightning coming off his fingertips.

I was Born of Water, Tobachischin, cooling the burnt hills of Santa Fe with soft gentle rain.

And there was Dan in the same dream, the boy I once knew and taught to write cool sentences. He had feathers of a red-tail hawk in his hair. His hands were feathered claws and they were wrapped around a can of beans.

Chapter Twenty-Three

Dan came to me from out of his dreamtime into mine.

"Run with me," he said.

I went with him into a tunnel like the bore of a rifle.

He was the power-runner. I the old teacher with the bum right leg—such as it is in real life. I tried to keep up with him.

We arrived at the tunnel's end. The bore, opening into blinding silver sun, was too bright for my eyes. But not for Dan's. He sprinted out of the tunnel, stopping to look back. "Come on," he said. "You can do it."

"I can't. The sun's too bright out there."

He shrugged, waved, said, "Next time then."

I woke, my heart pounding, tears in my eyes.

I had known Dan since he was a ninth-grade kid and I'd seen him grow into a world class runner competing in some of the nation's finest and most competitive 1500s. And he had filled a wall or two with awards and honors.

In the dream he vanished into the lances of sunlight, and into the roar of silence leaving me in the bore of a starting gun, unable to do anything.

Awake in the early morning, Laura still asleep by my side, I went back in time to the 1980s when Dan was hit by a car. I was there and saw it happen. It was exactly like the dream only in reverse. In reality, we went together in an ambulance to St Vincent's hospital. We didn't know then if he'd ever run again.

A year went by and Dan healed. But we still didn't know if he'd run again.

It was around that time that Laura and I went with Dan, his father and trainer, Fred, wife Debby and Dan's little brother Brendan. We traveled in our Toyota camper and Fred's Volkswagen camper to the Mexican Baja.

It was there I saw a saguaro cactus burst into flame in the desert and I wrote a poem for Dan which I called "The Prophecy".

I know you have doubts
        how this will go.
You'll pass them all, one by one
until
you stand alone
atop a stubble-bearded hill.

For I have seen it in the firelit saguaro,
        one finger of fire
            pointed up
one fist of flame
on the finish line.

Dan healed and became whole and the years passed, and he went on to fulfill that mystic prophecy of mine. In the end, there was no competitor left for him to vanquish. He'd beaten every distance runner in the U.S.

Thinking back, still feeling the dream of the tunnel and the bright light, I somehow tasted the desert salt of the Baja, and saw Dan again as a boy, not the grown, seasoned man that I ran with in the tunnel.

That man knew me, as I knew him.

And the tunnel … Jay told me about that once. A hole in a great rock in Crownpoint through which one can pass from this world to the next.

***

The rest of the day moved in synchrony with my dream. Which is to say, magically.

The pebble on the banco was gone.

In the days that followed, I painted a succession of three pebbles. The fourth pebble, Jay said, would return the harmony to our sky house apartment.

That day of the fourth pebble, Jay said, "Those who are lost sometimes see an old man with a blue face. But first, they see a small blue bird. Look for the old man at dusk. The bluebird may come at dawn. Either one, or both, will take you home."

"I understand," I told him. "But what of the pebble?"

"The fourth pebble enforces the laws of nature that can't be written in sand."

That night I walked along the coyote fence and for some reason I peeked through the cottonwood cracks, and there he was!

He wore a flat brim cowboy hat with a pinch at the crown. His eyes, deep set, showed his age as did his white, shoulder-length hair. His face was bluish in the dusky light. I saw the old man one moment, the next he was gone.

I climbed over the rough-bark fence and walked across the chamisa hollow to where the ruined, falling-down house cast shadows into the sunset. The front door was hanging by one rusted hinge. I poked my head inside. It was very dark in there.

I breathed the strange odors that hovered at the shadowed entryway.

They were a combination of fecal matter and dead flesh, or so it seemed. There was a rottenness, a detritus, overall that was unbreathable. My eyes burned. The longer I looked, standing in the doorway, the more I realized what was in there. On the far end of the deserted, dirt-floored old house, there were stacks of bodies. Human and animal forms in various wooden poses, frozen. Then, suddenly, and crazily, I threw up. It was as if my stomach just pitched everything out at once in a stream of vomit. It hit my running shoes in a wallop of filth.

At the same time, framed by the jagged broken window on my left, I saw the blue face again. "You better leave now," the old man said. "There's more than death in here. There's poisoned air."

After saying this, the blue face faded, disappeared.

As the old man melted from view, the fat, square face of Tony Appleplum appeared. Then, no more than a second later, he was on top of me. I was under his heavy body, being crushed by his weight.

I couldn't move anything but my eyes. Over Appleplum's head a white dove appeared, fluttering in the raftered darkness fifteen feet above the dirt floor of the fetid house.

"There is my chance," I thought.

I willed my left hand to tremble, and it did that thing. Appleplum brought his wide mouth down to mine. He was kissing me.

I tasted the vomit of my own lips and felt this same rancid saliva return from Appleplum's frogmouth to mine. He seemed to enjoy it. His eyes glowed.

Then as I was about to heave again—my hand went wild, and I trembled airborne. One swift vibration out of my body into the white dove on the rafter.

I looked down from the dove's eyes. I—the thing that was me—was still under Appleplum, pinned but no longer writhing. I had not seen this before. I was up above with bird's wings and I was down below under the block stone body of Appleplum.

I saw myself de-materialize. I faded, was gone on the ground, but was fully attentive to myself in the body of the dove.

Appleplum got to his feet and looked down at the soft dent in the earth where he'd pinned me. "Where are you?" he said into the darkness.

I glanced at the window. The blue face man was back. "Change again," he said.

Appleplum began ransacking the dead, cordwood bodies, looking for me. He overturned a wooden barrel of stiff rigamortis rats. He raged in a jumbled language that made no sense. "Come back puke lips," he cried. I understood that, all right, but kept perfectly still on the rafter. The shadows covered me like a shroud. I was hidden but the blue face protector, my guardian, told me again, "Change now into the owl."

I saw the owl as soon as he said the name. It was a barn owl, the kind with the questioning monkey face.

In a trembling of wings, I changed, and the owl was mine.

I felt the full breadth of feathers, the solid weight of a predatory animal.

"Strike!" said the old man at the window.

I did. Dropped hard and fast, open-taloned.

My spread claws raked Appleplum's face.

I heard him scream as I glided through the broken window, right over the head of the old man.

Then I soared upward into the cold burn of stars.

Appleplum's screams got fainter as the starlight grew brighter.

I landed on the railing of our balcony. The change began.

It started with the head—three-quarter owl, one quarter human. Then the quick tick of bones turning from pliant pin-feather to steely bone. After this the change accelerated. The heart beats faster as it exits body of bird, leaving behind the tawny whisper of taloned owl.

In the change, the five-chambered heart and the five-fingered hand are felt and formed. Gradually, as the familiar human host returns, one phase at a time, the body temperature alters. I was then a shivering thing of flesh, flat feet planted, nakedly alert in the changing air of first light.

In the distance, I heard the wail of a wounded animal.

Chapter Twenty-Four

Later, the following day, there was a soft knock at the door.

Not Mick who knocks hard.

Not Gabriela who taps.

But rather our other, downstairs neighbor, Susie.

"We could use your help," she said. "There's a poisonous snake at the top of the hill."

I threw on my jacket and went up to the complex of apartments on the hill near us. There was a crowd gathered around the topmost patio. I saw the snake right away. It had coiled and prepared to strike. A man said, "I'm going to get my gun." Another said, "I'm going to get my shovel." It seemed like the scene from Young Frankenstein where the monster is in the tower and the townspeople have gotten their pitchforks and lit their torches.

The snake was triangular-headed, buff colored and with a diamond pattern. Its tail was flickering and buzzing. I was about one foot away from striking distance and I stepped back a few paces and began to talk to the snake. It raised and cocked its head.

My back was toward the mumbling group of people. I got down on one knee and continued my whispering, while also trembling with my left hand.

The more calming energy I put into my hand, the lower the snake's head dropped. Soon, coils no longer present, the animal was lying straight out, preparatory to sliding off on its own. I didn't want it to do that. I also didn't want to scare it and have it coil up again. Most important, I didn't want to get bitten.

I began to actually whisper, telling the snake, "I will not hurt you. If you will let me, I will take you to somewhere safe." The snake remained motionless.

The golden-brown creature seemed less scared, so I continued to whisper. My hand was now close enough to touch it, but I knew I could retract my hand as fast as I needed to if it should turn on me.

The tail rattling stopped.

I moved my hand even closer.

Then I picked up its upper body—my left hand just below its head—as my right hand took its lower length. The snake came away from the wall willingly and wrapped several coils around my forearm.

I turned and passed through the crowd. Naturally they parted giving me room. I saw the man with the gun, the man with the shovel and two women in Army uniforms. I walked to the coyote fence that was nearest to us, and let it go through a crack in the cedar poles. The snake uncoiled and easing itself through the crack disappeared until all I could see was its tail.

That was when I found out that it was a non-poisonous bullsnake. They do that, bullsnakes do, they imitate rattlers when frightened. It fooled me.

I returned to the apartment with the blood singing in my ears. As I came in through the front door, the phone rang. It was Jay. Figures, I thought.

"Pebbles still there?" he asked.

"The fourth one is still there."

He chuckled. "Does it have the stars?"

"Yes,"

"So what happened last night?" he wanted to know.

"Were you there, Jay?"

He didn't answer.

"The blue man," I said. "He helped me."

"The one who takes you home. Did he?"

"He did. In a way. He definitely saved me."

"And now?"

"I just saved some folks who were prepared to kill a snake. I mean, I just saved a snake from some scared people who wanted to kill it."

Jay laughed. "Snakes are our friends. But a man can have too many friends sometimes. Anyone get bitten?"

"No."

"And," he pursued, "the snake is safe and on its way home?"

I told him that the snake and the people were in their own worlds now. I added, "No one got hurt."

"That's good. What about the sickos next door?"

I sighed. "They're here. But they've been given their notice."

"Who gave it to them?" he asked.

"The blue man and me plus a dove and an owl."

Chapter Twenty-Five

We decided to take a quick trip into the mountains to see if it would shed some of the madness that had burned its way into our lives.

We drove north to Sapello.

Our long ago, faraway place. The village where we'd met fifty years ago. It always calmed the nerves to be there.

It boggled the mind to think that an entire half-century ago a brown-eyed boy and a green-eyed girl had fallen in love in these same incorruptible memory mountains of the Southwest.

After driving for several hours, we arrived at our destination in the ponderosa pines and stopped at a roadside bar. I drank a toast to my good left hand, or whatever source of magic commanded and made it work. I have always wondered what it all means … I still do.

Laura is always quiet about what she doesn't understand, and she definitely didn't understand hand trembling beyond the obvious—the Navajos did it and it worked for them. But she'd seen it work for me, too, and she was always there when I was learning the ancient hand patterns and prayers.

So we were up there in the mountains where we first held hands, both of us thankful for all that was and would be, and hopeful that things would get so much better. It was at that moment, a few sips into our chile beers, when a man seated one elbow away at the bar fell over in slow motion, his eyes closed, his head wearily weaving to the polished wood.

The woman next to him put her ear to his chest and said, "He's gone. Poor Fritz is dead."

We moved as if in a dream. I got up from where I sat, a second man joined me in removing poor Fritz from the bar, and we carried him to a comfortable chair over by the fireplace.

Within moments the place swarmed with EMTs and firemen.

Fritz had his blood pressure checked. The lady who did this couldn't get a good reading, she said. She kept trying and shaking her head.

I stood back and thought about the trembling unconscious man whose heartbeat had come back but was not steady. It was still very faint.

Then, some minutes after, I changed my mind.

Maybe I could do something to help. Jay used to tell me that, aside from hand trembling and divining and other things, there was silent prayer, and beyond that, or in addition to that, just standing or sitting in the presence of someone struggling to live, can help.

I had once come out of a bad situation because Jay and three of his friends—so many years ago—had sat in a hospital waiting for me to waken after surgery. They sat. Merely sat. No prayers. Nothing but silent sitting. Even today I still feel their presence in that room. There is power in not doing anything. In not rushing nervously about—in not doing too much and not being afraid of doing too little.

Fritz woke up, got his steady heartbeat back, and lived to drink another day.

We drove on to the little cabin in rumpled, humpbacked hills of Sapello.

This was the same territory where we had seen a UFO, and where time stopped, and started again, and then rolled over and repeated itself.

Driving up the steep mountain road, we saw another one of those polly-wogs born of fire from afar, and stopped to watch it trail off into the pines. A cumulous cloud of smoke rose up, and a final flare and then the night took over as it always does in remote places, snuffing out even the memory of light.

Why does this always happen? I asked myself.

Chapter Twenty-Six

"What was it?" I asked Laura as we walked up the mountain road.

"You would like me to say it wasn't a meteor, it was a UFO," she answered.

We were walking steadily up the windy road to the cabin. In the ponderosa dark there was no moon, no friendly lamp glow from a cabin window. The cabins we passed on our way looked abandoned, desolate. Up ahead in the weak starlight we saw the old cabin in the pine needle scrub night.

"What did the thing look like to you?" I asked her. We were almost to the cabin now; one turn and we'd be there.

"A meteor."

Later that night, safely tucked into the upstairs bed, we went to sleep listening to wind chimes on the porch.

I woke before first light. Checked my watch: 4:55 AM. The moment I open my eyes in the night, I am awake. It's a curse, a blessing, a trait. Nothing I can do about it.

Laura got up and went down the steep stairs to the bathroom. A moment, then the flush, then the soft steps coming up the stairs.

She got into bed but strangely her skin was still bed-warm. How could that be? The cabin was pretty cold.

A couple minutes passed while I lay awake and thought about this.

Then Laura got up, same way as before, and went down the stairs again.

This time I got up and waited for her. It was goose-bump chilly, probably in the low 40s somewhere.

"You feeling OK?" I asked as she returned to bed.

"Can't a girl go to the bathroom?"

"I saw you do the same thing twice."

She pulled the quilt up to her chin. "It's dark morning, too early to argue. I only went to the bathroom once. You must've been dreaming."

"But I wasn't. I swear I saw you go up and down twice."

"Are you crazy?" she whispered, already drifting back into sleep.

She slept.

I lay awake thinking about things.

Laura was a rationalist. I wasn't. I accepted phenomena as some kind of normal, whether outrageous, unbelievable, or totally comprehensible. Laura lived on another plane. She saw things differently. Rarely emotionally. Mostly factually.

I recalled Etienne and his insistence that "If you see a UFO, and afterwards you begin seeing other things that are in the wrong order of occurrence, this is proof that you saw a UFO."

"I can accept that," I told him.

Then he said, "Can you embrace the time/space/continuum?"

"I've never quite understood what that was, even though, linguistically, it does make sense. It's warped time, right?"

Etienne laughed. "Do you know Marcel Duchamp's Cubist painting called Nude Descending A Staircase? It's as if he painted a kind of Cubistic phantom, where you see each movement of her body as it's in descent. A jittery newsreel that confounds the human eye."

"How does a UFO sighting and a painting by a mid-century French artist compare? Is there any connection, really?"

"Definitely. We see things often in cinema-like hesitation. Like looking out of a car window, the car being in motion, and you viewing objects outside the car. At that very moment, you have what I call 'Cubist eye vision'."

"That's a lot," I told him, "to take in, but I get it."

He went on. "You see in a stop-motion experiential way. Dot, dot, dot. Like that. Very quick eye pulsations. After you've seen a UFO, people who saw it say they experienced just that kind of visionary thing. A bizarre motion effect. Maybe that is really just Reality with a capital R. Maybe animals see that way most of the time. Especially horses and birds, I have been told."

This conversation happened thirty-five years before this night in the cabin. How had I even remembered it? I lay awake, thinking more about Cubism, Etienne, Laura, rationality, UFOs. Lying in bed in the pre-dawn light, it all made perfect sense. But I knew the puzzle pieces would fly apart and roost in the subconscious in the light of day.

My mind took me back to the sight of the cordwood bodies stacked in the deadhouse in Santa Fe. Had I really seen them? Were they a flash image in altered time? Was I, myself, in an altered state as a result of the trembling? Was it all a stop-motion experience of some kind? Like my imaginings as a child, when I would go into the "secret closet."

I surely trembled things at age five. But I had no idea where I was going or what I was doing. I only knew that my left hand trembled me into a magical reality, so that the closet itself melted away, and I found myself in a land of six-dimensional possibility. A land of Oz.

For years my mother tried to discourage me from this destructive—she thought—activity. A medical doctor had witnessed me doing it, a result of my mother's concern. His diagnosis was that I was perhaps entering an incipient phase of schizophrenia. Not only that, but because he'd observed how I held the fingers of my left hand so near to my eyes, he feared I might, in the course of time, go cross-eyed. Or worse, completely blind.

Well, it was the mid-1940s. He probably didn't know what to make of it. I still don't.

I never know if what I do, and see, is, as the kids like to say, real.

Chapter Twenty-Seven

Laura and I returned to The Veranda the next evening. On the way back into Santa Fe, we stopped at Harry's Roadhouse for a mahi-mahi red chile sandwich. We ordered a bottle of Predator red, a dry, piquant Zinfandel sold hardly anywhere but Harry's.

Then we bustled on to our apartment. We were met at the bottom of the stairs by Gabriela who greeted us with a hurricane of news and enthusiasm. "Where have you two escapees been?"

"We were up in—"

"So, listen," she began, "can you guess what went on while you were gone?"

"We saw a UFO."

This time it was Laura who cut in. "Maybe a meteor."

"Of course you did. UFO, by the look in your eyes. But anyway, guess who skipped town." Gabriela pursed her lips. Secret time.

I said, "Could it be Mr. Appleplum?"

"You knew," Gabriela said and her mouth opened in surprise. "I'm supposed to be the one who knows everything," she chided. But listen: No kidding, that bird has flown!"

Gabriela's cat-green eyes were illumined with excitement. As I stared into them, I understood all over again why she was a licensed psychic. Those eyes of sea foam green, of Caribbean mystery untold could capture a frog and turn him into a prince—for a price!

"Do tell," Laura urged. "Are you sure he left … was it just him?"

Gabriela rolled her eyes and swept us both with a deep, penetrating sea-wash of intrigue. "He departed at 4:45 AM. That's this morning."

"All of them?" Laura asked doubtfully.

"The whole kit and caboodle," Gabriela said with emphasis. Jeff and I saw it all out our slider, with the curtain mostly drawn of course, but we could see how they safaried out of here, and guess who didn't carry a single thing?"

"The Girl?" Laura said.

"That would be incorrect," Gabriela said, laughing.

"Then—who?" I wondered aloud.

"I want to tell you, that little bitty pretty girl carried box after box along with that smartass brother of hers, if that's what he is, Jeff and I are doubtful. Maybe none of the bitches are related but that's beside the point. They're gone, tee hee."

She actually said that old comic book line. Then she inhaled deeply, looked around and continued. "So I did some more research on them using Jeff's Lexus Nexus and some connections I have who will remain anonymous, but anyway, the wifey, if that's what she is, and I very much doubt it, changed her name, changed all of their names in fact, legally, and they're all monikered as Smith. Can you imagine? The Appleplum-Smith family, sounds like a phony stage name, right? Like a bunch of characters in Mary Poppins, for god's sake, but let's give them that because …"

She held us in suspense right there in the courtyard of The Veranda. Then blasted it out so every apartment could hear—"THEY'RE GONE!"

She then whispered, "No more fucking all hours of the night oh I'm so going to love going to sleep and not waking until I fucking feel like it … no more hump-hopping that poor little waify, no more standing beating off with wifey, no more …what do you think the bad little boy was doing while this shit was going on?"

"Watching," Laura said.

"And no more fuckingwatching," Gabriela said.

She leaned very close. Encircling both of us with her wide-reaching arms.

"There's one more guess-what with the Appleplum departure."

"Let's see," Laura said. "Could it be they left without paying their rent?"

"Now, how in the world did you know?" Gabriela asked.

"It figures," Laura said.

"OK," Gabriela said, breathing heavily, "there's one more thing because there's always one more thing with such people—and why am I calling them people, I don't have any idea? —do you know I never thought they were human, never believed so, ask Jeff, he didn't believe either, but not to beat a dead horse, there's still one more thing … but I'm not going to tell you, you have to go upstairs and see it for yourselves. It's just below the door. Above the door is the notice from Management saying their rent's overdue, tee hee."

After it was quite dark, I slipped through the crack in the coyote fence and went down to the deadhouse—that was one secret Gabriela might never uncover. On the other hand she might dream it all and tell us about it.

I entered the dreary place with my penlight.

Dreary is in fact too weak a word because that rotten adobe smelled of boiled bones, marrow leakage, major ammoniacal urine deposits, more horse than human, excrement of the fourth kind (extraterrestrial?), and all manner of foreign and unnamable odors. In all my life I only experienced smells similar to this once—on a tropic summer day in the highlands of Jamaica at a butcher's where horses were being killed and carved along with goats and pigs. After that day I became an instant vegan.

This was like that, only worse.

And to make matters worse, my penlight scanned the dust and there directly in front of me was a goat's head, recently severed, dripping with gore. There was a folded note attached to one of the curly horns. I opened it and it was a crayon scrawl with these words:

Hey, Lucky Ducky,
No time for plucky
Next time,
Plenty fucky, Bucky.

I was still seeing that message and smelling the foulness of deadhouse, after I got to the top of the stairs at The Veranda. As I started to open our door, I turned and glanced at the banco. The star pebble was gone.

Then remembering what Gabriela had said, I walked over to the Appleplum's door and looked downward. My penlight shone on the welcome mat where there was a child's version of skull and crossbones done in magic marker. Below that, a giant hairy dick and balls.

Chapter Twenty-Eight

Laura and I fell asleep as soon as our heads hit the pillow. But, first, we listened to the wailing wall that connected us to Appleplum-Smith's apartment.

Nothing there but silence.

Silent, sibilant, nothingness.

Delectable emptiness.

For six months we'd heard nightly rages of bedsprings. Sexting, groaning, scraping, sighing and sawing. We'd tossed and turned listening to a cacophony of whining, screaming, crying, grunting, and the theatrical orations of a Roman senator, the maniacal laughter of a feral clown, the orgasms of a teenager in love with her father, and the pig whistles of a wife in love with herself and a cucumber.

And now it was over. The theater company had left.

There was a hole in the universe of absurdity.

And we filled it with blessed, blissful, beautiful, harmonic sleep.

***

The following day and evening I spent with Laura trying to figure out what was happening. One day after the "Smiths" went on their way, I got a call from an agent of mine asking if I would like to write a series of true stories for a magazine called Wyrd.

That is, the old Anglo-Saxon word for our commonly misunderstood word, weird.

"How true is true?" I asked my agent.

She replied, "How true do you want it to be? You're the writer."

"How about very, very true?"

"As long as it's weird, they don't care what you write. The editor is an avid reader of yours, by the way."

"I knew I had at least one."

She didn't say anything for a moment, then, "I checked this morning … you have 586,000 online iterations for that quote we gave to IBM and NPR and some other organizations for free."

"It's the free part that makes me feel so much better," I said.

"To eat you must have food," she quipped. "To write you must have sponsors. In this mendacious age of ours, when worth is measured by gross national product, we have to make concessions. Those concessions are called giveaways so we can later benefit from take-aways."

"I'm not complaining," I answered. "What's the editor's email address."

She gave it to me. It was an address in Canada. By the time I actually got around to phoning her, the editor, who was a very nice sounding, sweet woman with no agenda except quality, she said, I got the job as a stringer.

"How did you find me?" I asked.

"Internet," she confided. "A little quote of yours popularly known up here as The Wolf Quote. Your name actually came up with Aldo Leopold, Hal Borland, Mother Teresa, Bob Marley, Madeleine L'Engle, Patricia Dale-Green, Hilary Hemingway, Terry Tempest Williams, M. Oldfield Howey, and Homer Simpson."

"So my bribe to Homer worked!"

"Oh, by the way, you can be funny, if you want to be in your articles and none of them need to be more than 1,200 words..."

"—I'm in," I said. And to Laura, as soon as I got off the phone: "I got a job!"

She came in to my study and said, "I heard that. Congrats on saving our ship. We were taking on some water, did you know?"

"Whenever Dan tells me I'm full of beans and mice sing in our kitchen, I know we've got a leak somewhere."

She gave me her almost-smile, then said, "Seriously, I just got an email from a lawyer I'd written to months ago in Manhattan who's added us to a class action suit based on that property of ours that was gobbled up by Wells-Fargo."

"What could that possibly bring?"

"If we ever get it … hmm, hard to believe, but he said each party in the suit should receive around ten thousand dollars."

"Could it be our luck is changing?"

Laura shook her head. "The weight of Applescum lifts, and you get a job and I get an email that could erase six months of woe, and who knows what might happen next …"

"I'd settle for a little solvency," I said.

"So would I."

***

That evening we decided to celebrate our two unrelated, unanticipated, unbelievable events. I drove to Papa Murphy's and bought one of their plain cheese pizza doughs and we brought it back to the apartment and Laura started dressing it up with chile and olives prior to putting it in the oven.

I was about to open a bottle of wine when I heard a scratch at the door.

Tony Apple-Plum-Smith already?

I answered the door and there was a panting black DOG.

"May I come in?" he said.

I was surprised. Laura standing beside me was astonished.

I'd told her about Al-lan in a dog suit before, but this appearance, in the fur, so to say, stopped her, as it would anyone.

Once in, Al-lan said, in that unctuous, pleasing voice of his, "May I please remove this stinking hot doggy outfit?"

He did that thing in the bathroom and came out with loose dog fur all over his homeless person's gray shirt that was once upon a time perhaps white. He was a small, wan-faced man in need of a shower and a shave and some decent clothes and a meal and who knows what else.

Before we could even ask him to dine with us, he begged a shower.

Laura put the pizza in the oven. "A little man in a dog suit," she mumbled.

"More luck … or something else?"

"Luck," I said. "This guy's the original four-leaf clover."

While Al-lan showered, Laura and I picked out some clothes of hers that would fit him. They, he and Laura, were about the same size, medium woman.

He stepped out in a towel wrap and said, "Look, Ma, no paws!" He looked squeaky clean, except for his face. His skin was faintly blue, but I could see he had just shaved.

Was he the blue man Jay had mentioned?

The blue bird legendary savior of the Navajo, the one who sorts out lost souls, and who saved me in the deadhouse?

Was it Al-lan all along?

Chapter Twenty-Nine

Al-lan in his present form was nothing much to look at. You would not notice him on the street, in a parking lot, in front of the supermarket. I guessed he liked it that way.

"Life is better as a dog," he told us. "Especially if you only appear at night when humans see poorly."

We ate the Papa Murphy's pizza upon which Laura had conferred some fresh roasted Hatch chile, some black olives and anchovies. The cheese was already on the dough. We ate, Al-lan ate, our parrot George, of whom I will say more later, ate, keeping up with the rest of us. Sometimes besting us with his efficient and timely beak.

"Did I see any of that stuff in that broken-down adobe that we call Dead-house? Or did I sort of make it up?"

Al-lan grinned. He had fairly bad teeth, and was missing more than he had, but he liked his pizza and that was a good thing. "I would have to ask you that question—Did you make it up? Or does the eye make it up? Which is it?"

"Maybe neither," I said.

"That is a good answer," he said, washing his pizza down with a glass of merlot. "We don't really know because the eye is such an imperfect mechanism. The brain more imperfect than the eye. Then, too, you humans are so suggestible that anything the mind suggests the eye seems to see, at one time or another. And in reverse what the eye suggests, the mind delights in manifesting. So, my friends, there you are … a human conundrum."

"Is that why you resort to the shape of an animal?" Laura questioned.

Al-lan nodded, smiled, put away another slice. A piece of chile dangled off his lip. He seemed unaware of it. But, of course, he was only recently drawn out of his dogskin and fur. He chewed like a dog, too. Fast and furious, as if he'd never see another meal like this one. Maybe that was true.

"Your own science seems to suggest that animals such as cats and dogs see in ultraviolet light. You know that, don't you?"

"I've read that," Laura stated. "Is it true?"

Al-lan grinned, gap-toothed, and chuckled. "You think I know?"

Laura and I both shrugged.

"Dr Frey thought you knew practically everything."

"Except how to drive a car," Laura put in.

"I'm still not good at it," he said, continuing to eat and grin at the same time.

"What are you good at?" Laura persisted.

"Eating," Al-lan mumbled with a mouthful of pizza.

"How do you help humanity?" Laura asked.

"I don't."

I asked him how Dr Frey, who was a reliable scientist, believed that he, Al-lan, was an ascended being from outer space.

"There is no outer space," he answered. "There is nothing but space."

"What about the solar system?"

"Forget about it," Al-lan grumbled, and swallowed. He took another glass of wine and downed it like water. "Look," he said, "how far we've wavered from our original conversation which was sight. You might ask me why dogs and cats can see spirit matter, ghosts, intraterrestrials, extraterrestrials, whatever. UV light is a wave, like everything else humans respond to, but it's beyond the red to violet sight in their repertoire. Human eye lenses block the UV that animals see as a matter of course. But what earlier science said, people believed. That is, the idea that animals couldn't see UV. Now you know what I mean when I say that human beings are very suggestible. Dogs are that way, too, because humans taught them to be that way. Cats to a much lesser degree because their inclination is not follow human dictates, but rather to be inclined to follow their own."

For a good little while, no one said anything.

Al-lan kept eating and licking his fingers. "I haven't eaten corporeal food in a long time," he said apologetically. "It's really something. But I have to say the way it's eliminated—" he patted his butt and laughed—"that's a task I wouldn't want to indulge in. It's both time consuming and spiritually enervating. Waste of time, frankly."

"Do aliens … I mean to say, people from outerspace … I mean other galaxies," Laura commented, "excrete, well, differently?"

"Some drop loads," if that's what you mean. Some don't. On Xerxes where I used to live the beings among whom and some I associated, farted with their mouths."

"They must've had awful breath," I suggested.

"Quite the contrary. They smelled like lilacs in spring. Or honey fresh from the comb. Their thoughts actually produced their farts, not their bellies."

Laura looked surprised. "What did their bellies do?"

Al-lan said, "You ask a lot of questions for such a cute lady. But, to answer your query, the truth is, they'd long ago lost bellyness altogether. I mean to say, they had no need of digestion. You know, it's kind of a silly idea. The ultimate purpose is to have mind. Mind is everything."

"There is such a thing as mind farts," I mentioned.

Al-lan said, "Keep those to yourself, if you don't mind … by the way that's one thing other civilizations in the great galactic scheme of things, seem to have lost."

"What have they lost?" I pursued.

"The language arts. You know, where words mean many different things and can thus be played with. You know, folks, I've got to go, I have to make sure those plum people got to their destination and won't come back to haunt you."

"I thought you said you didn't do anything for humanity."

"I don't. I'm doing it for you."

"Why is that?" I asked.

"You've been nice to me. You even put me in a book. We, I mean Xerxians, don't do that anymore. Let me ask you this …" He looked me in the eyes. "Are you going to put me into any more of your books?"

"I am," I said, "I can promise you that."

Al-lan grinned, then burst out laughing. "That's another thing we've lost," he said.

"What is?" I begged to know.

"Laughter," he said. "You won't find much of that anywhere in the humdrum universes I travel to and from. It's serious stuff they're about. They've mostly gotten rid of the encumbrance of war, but then, they're humorless as hell."

"There's ... hell?" Laura said, surprised.

"Always was, always will be. Mostly make-believe though. No one really worries about it, but it is like going to a party full of stuffed shirts."

"Couldn't you stay and talk some more," Laura said.

"The Plums, remember?"

"Pummel the Plums then," she said.

"Actually," he said, "they're pretty funny."

Chapter Thirty

I got a call from my old friend Will Channing, owner of Wings of the Southwest Gallery. Will and I had known each other for many years going back to when he owned a small gallery in West Stockbridge, Massachusetts. He was trading in American Indian art and I had just completed my first book for a major publisher. The book, *Sitting on the Blue-Eyed Bear*, was a collection of Navajo legends told to me by Jay DeGroat. The year was 1975.

"How's the writing going?" Will asked.

"I'm working for a magazine in Canada," I told him, and explained the kinds of things I'd be covering.

"Well," he said, "Come over to the gallery, I've some things downstairs in the basement that might warrant your attention."

"Like what?"

"Edward S. Curtis material. Photographs from just before the turn of the last century, for one thing, and for another … it's a little hard to explain on the phone but I've acquired a collection from Ellwood Burris Barnes. There's stuff in there that might warrant a story or two. You're welcome to take a peek whenever you have time."

A few days later, I was in an elevator in the Catron Building, descending to Will's basement where the mysterious collection was piled up in boxes. It seemed a bit helter-skelter for what Will told me it was worth. Along with the Curtis prints of Navajo and Pueblo Indians, the materials in banker's boxes, there were rugs, blankets, even squash blossom necklaces hanging on wooden mannikins.

I stepped out of the cranky old elevator that hadn't been serviced since 1888 and Will said, "I have an appointment. Just look around as much as you want. I'll be back in fifteen minutes."

As the ancient elevator complained and creaked back up to the third floor, I took stock of the basement. It had an earthen smell. Piles of cipher paper littered one end, I saw some bronze figures, green with age, a beautiful

Buddha, and a wooden Indian with hand outstretched clutching a bunch of hundred year old cigars.

Then the lights went out. Even the elevator light. I heard footsteps on the first-floor tongue-and-groove flooring above, and then little else.

My immediate thought was: What the hell am I doing here?

Then: I can't see anything. It was as pitch dark as when they turned out the lights in Carlsbad Caverns to show what the complete absence of light was.

I stood awkwardly, waiting for the lights to come on.

But they didn't.

For a moment or two, I breathed deeply, reassuring myself that very, very soon the lights would pop on, and I'd be doing what I was supposed to be doing—searching for a story amidst the myriad banker's boxes.

I told myself that the elevator was behind me. The collection was in front of me. On either side there was nothing but empty space, leading to what I had noticed was rock walls from the century, or centuries, before.

I asked myself then what animal would be comfortable in so much untextured darkness, and I decided a cat would like it here. This thought passed rather quickly. Catlike, I took a step forward and touch something.

It felt damp and toothy. An animal? Was it alive?

The mind plays tricks in the dark.

And when the dark is absolute and unforgiving, the dark soon becomes an enemy to reckon with.

I forced myself to inspect what I hadn't seen when the lights were on.

It was, in fact, my fingers told me, a piece of primitive New Mexico sculpture.

A pig with rows of peg-like teeth.

I relaxed and told my heart to do the same. Imagine being afraid of a piece of folk art. I chuckled to myself.

But this basement seemed to have a kind of force field. It held you and released you. I felt walls moving, entrapping, moving yet again, dissolving, materializing again. A shiver passed along my spine and I shook it off.

How much time has gone by since the lights shut down?

Minutes? Certainly not more than twenty of them.

Here I was, I thought, in the Underworld. The sipapu. The place of beginnings. The People, the Diné, had come from this primordia and had risen through the help of First Man, Heron, Locust and others, to the fourth world, which was the one we know full of air and light.

The Hero Twins, much later, had cleansed the fourth world of monsters that had also come from the first world, but the monsters had not evolved. If anything they had seemed to devolve. So Nayenezgani, the great mythical warrior, had killed giant lizards, enormous winged and fanged bats, poisonous reptiles of all kinds, not to mention deformed spiders and crazy ants that ate people. There were more monsters than one could name. It was also Heron, the Helper, who brought some of these monsters into the light of the upper world, reasoning that even evil has a place in the firmament. Dark stars roamed the skies and caused more death and destruction and there was chaos everywhere. But Nayenezgani and his brother Tobachischin cleansed the earth of these aberrations and the world began anew.

But—no matter the force of good, no matter the right intentions of the brothers—evil was an equally palpable force and Coyote, the good and bad brother of all of us, played his part in actualizing the ancient creatures that preferred night to day, and evil to good. It is believed that some of these are still with us.

I thought of these things and then expunged them from my thinking and concentrated on some form of escape. I needed to get out. With some effort I reversed my position, facing, I hoped, the elevator door. Then I walked, somewhat confidently with my hands in front of me.

The cold metal door was not as near as I thought. I had to pat the block walls with open palms, moving ever to the left.

Finally I made it to metal, and patted that and there was a ringing sound that came from the chamber that I knew was elevator.

I began, then, to beat a soft steady rhythm.

Surely someone on the first floor might hear this. In any case, I kept doing it, over and over, louder and louder.

No one came. Nothing happened. No lights blinked. I stopped drumming.

It came to me when I stopped pounding that a much longer passage of time had elapsed. Will had left me long ago. Maybe an hour. Maybe two. I was trapped in cold hell looking for a cask of Amontillado. This random thought a gift from my childhood reading of Edgar Allan Poe.

All right then … what was I to do?

I felt the walls undulating like water plants.

Then it came to me … if I ever wanted to get out of this place … for what if something had happened to Will? What if … what if no one knew I was down here … what ifs stormed my brain. But then, as I said, it came to me. If, by chance, there was a life form, a corporeal life form, in the basement, I could tremble myself into it, and use this creature, whatever it might be, to escape.

I now felt the walls resisting this thought. They came closer.

I trembled harder than I can ever remember trembling. I circled back to when I was a child hidden in the closet. My heart began to skip beats. Then it went on a tangent of patterns, skipping, skipping. I gasped for air. My left hand fluttered and I felt the weight and strength come into it as I soared from my stationary place into the body of something.

It was as if I'd run hard into it. I was inside it. And it was something living. Something alive.

But what?

The trembling had stopped cold. I was there. I was where?

Words came into my mind. "Touch me. I am here. Feel my chest."

I did this thing. Cold metallic buttons.

There was an infinitesimal stirring within the life form.

It can think, I thought.

"Who are you?" I asked.

"Feel my face," it said.

From within the chamber of its body, I attempted to move my hands, but I had no hands, and I knew this.

"I can't feel you, I'm in you," I said.

"As I am in you. We are in one another."

"I have never been so afraid," I said. "I have no control."

"Neither do I," came the voice.

"Are you … Al-lan … testing me?"

"I am not."

"Are you dead?"

"I was, until you came into me," the voice said.

"How do we get out of here?" I asked, the fear rising in me like a suffocating tide.

"Where is here?" the voice asked reasonably.

"I am afraid," I said.

"What is afraid?"

"To have fear."

"What is fear?" I asked.

"Fear is what you are most afraid of in life" I said in a quavering voice.

There was a term of silence. Neither of us spoke. Then the voice said, "What is life?"

I answered with a line I once read that Sitting Bull said: "Life is a firefly on a summer night."

Then I felt a sudden rush of power come into my limbs, if limbs they were. And I trembled everywhere—arms, hands, knees, legs, even my face tingled with some flickering semblance of life.

"Say it again," the voice said.

I repeated, "Life is a firefly on a summer night."

"Once, long ago, I said that," the voice said. "I remember it now. I remember who I was."

"Who were you?"

"I am Sitting Bull," the voice said.

At that moment, the doors of the elevator ground their teeth and grumbled.

The lights sputtered on, making a fizzing sound.

There was a deep subterranean groan.

Steel doors shuddered.

Warm air shafted into the cool tunnel of coldness.

The upper world returned with a grating roar and a bash of glaring light.

"Sorry, old man, I'm a few minutes late, but still on schedule, I believe. And how did you make out down here in the catacombs. I heard that the lights went out for a minute or two."

It was Will who stood there before me. Tall as a chimney, straight as an oak, perfect Brit accent smooth as a tumbler of whiskey in the golden dawn of the first electric light. I was very glad to see him, so glad I gave him a hug.

He returned it with one of his own. "Did you find the Curtis prints?" he asked.

"I got sort of involved with that statue." "Samuel Taylor French," Will said. "I believe it's an early study he did. Some say it might be Sitting Bull, but again it could be Two Guns White Calf. No one knows for sure. We've got to come up with an assessment, maybe a provenance later. Want to do that for me?"

"I think I already have," I replied.

Chapter Thirty-One

Al-lan phoned the following morning. I didn't know he had a cellphone. Or my number. I'd given it to no one. It was just for outgoing. But, then, Al-lan is all about incoming, so there you have it.

"Just saw Tony Appleplum-Smith," Al-lan said.

"Where are you?"

"Currently? In Denver. That skip-the-rent rascal said he was going to Seattle, 'To the beach' was how I heard him say it."

"You heard him say that?"

"Overheard him. I'm a dog, remember?"

"Sometimes a blue-faced old man," I corrected.

"That's strictly for you and Laura. You know, the truth is, I like being a dog. The smells, the sounds. There's nothing like it. It gets confusing though—so many smells, so many sounds. Very distracting. And you're hungry almost all the time because odors of eating are wafting in front of your nose 24/7."

"Do you eat garbage?"

"Sometimes, just for the hell of it. It's not bad, actually. I go to the back of Burger King, for example, where they have those Dumpster things, and I just hop in and you'd be surprised how many perfectly good throw-aways there are in that iron box, I mean hundreds. It's like lined with hamburgers, cheeseburgers, bacon cheeseburgers, french fries, fish sandwiches."

"I don't need the whole menu. I was asking if you ate all that stuff."

"You mean," Al-lan asked, "do I indulge in all kinds of food festivities, or do I eat ALL the stuff in the Dumpster?"

"The latter ..."

There was a moment of silence.

"I eat all of it, I'm ashamed to say. I know, I know, humans don't do that, but there's the nice thing about being a dog. I can eat junk, real junk food, and then slip out of the box and no one's seen me and I am full up to my whiskers and I don't have to eat for another hour or so."

"You're not a dog, Al-lan, you're a pig!"

He barked. Woof, woof, woof. A laugh bark.

"Did you call my private number for a reason?"

"I wanted to tell you about your former neighbor. He told management at The Veranda that he was going to Seattle, and as I said, I overheard this. He was bragging to his wife that they were heading for the beach. Well, I lived in the Northwest for a while, I guess Dr Frey told you that. And there's beaches, but really crummy ones in Seattle. Not even beaches, really. Scum rocks with seaweed on them. I had his fake address—swiped it from that nerd Frankie at The Veranda. You know, the little Mexican in the pinstripe suit."

"You're not supposed to say, 'little Mexican' it's derogatory, demeaning and stupid."

"I can say anything I want, I'm not from around here. I'm from Xerxes. And that's a few trillion miles off in the interplay of subatomic matter, energy and photons, dark matter and electromagnetic forces you wouldn't understand if I explained it to you. If you consider though that a trillionth of a second has passed since the beginning of so-called Time, as you call it, well, anyway, you get the picture."

"It sounds like you've been listening to Neil deGrasse Tyson."

"Actually I've been reading him."

"How do you paw through those pages?"

"I have a Kindle, I swipe them with my paw."

"Where do you keep the Kindle? I didn't see it when you were visiting us."

"Well since you ask, I have this little barrel on a collar. I won it off a St Bernard in a card game."

"A St Bernard? The barrel must be huge!"

Barks again. And woofs.

Then: "It gets lost in my fur. That's an advantage, you know, being a very furry Retriever-Chow mix. I can store stuff in my coat and since it's pitch black, no one sees the half of it. Which reminds me, you've got to take me to one of those Barks and Bubbles, Critter's Corner places where you wash dogs and groom them squeaky clean."

"You could go blue face and wash your doggy suit. No one'll think anything of it. An eccentric old man with a dog blanket or something."

Al-lan sighed, and growled.

"Nothing's as easy as you make it seem. My blue face, as you put it, is not available by day."

"Oh, I see. Al-lan, I have a question: Why did you call?"

"You're right it wasn't just to chat about subatomic particles and E equals MC squared. I wanted to inform you that I'm on Tony's case. He's got a very degenerate plan."

I gagged a little. "You mean, banging his daughter?"

"No, not that. He seems to be moving mice around. Highly toxic little, cute little, singing mice that could, quite literally, destroy the world that you know and love. Or at least know and tolerate. Sorry, got to go. Call you back."

He didn't though.

He messaged me a poem and it went like this:

> There are so many things that you can't see, touch, smell, and taste.
> You are so busy using delete that you have eliminated de-light.
> Humans used to be aware of everything, and delight in everything.
> When was the last time you smelled new mown hay?
> You know the musty, rusty smell of roses?
> How about day old, mold gotten, sun-rotten meat?
> How about a can of whipped cream?
> How about salt off some seaweed at the beach? Real salt, not the stuff that comes in a shaker.
> What about a dead fly on a dusty windowsill? Ever smelled that?

How about the scent of falling snow or a fog sandwich from the sea?

How about the sound of pipes knocking in a distant house on a silent night?

What about the smell of a beautiful dog lady at a certain time of month?

How about the taste of bubblegum that has been creamed and toasted in the sun and then frosted in the cold and tastes like ancient toothpaste and old worn out stinky sneakers when you chew it?

These are all things I never knew I loved until I turned dog.

Sniff you later, pal. Gotta go again. I mean, really, I gotta go!

Chapter Thirty-Two

Every now and then we get an order for one of our Navajo books and sometimes it's a small school out on the reservation and their way of ordering and paying is off the grid, so to say. One afternoon, the man doing the ordering, Mr. Ambrose, from Pine Spring Elementary, phoned me saying, "We have no way of paying you for these books of yours unless you can accept a credit card from our school."

Laura explained that we couldn't do this because we were authors, not a retail business.

"Do you have twenty copies of *The Coyote Bead*?"

Laura said, "Yes, we do."

"Is there a trading post around where you live?"

"I think there is one that we have consigned books to on Cerrillos Road. Would that help?"

Mr. Ambrose said, "It could solve the problem."

So we drove over to Tin-Nee-Ann Trading Post where Jo, an old friend of ours, said she would look and see if she had any more copies of Bead. I told her that wasn't necessary, "We have twenty copies in the car and that's exactly the number this school wants to have."

"Well, bring them on in," Jo said. Then added, "You can think of this store as your warehouse." She laughed and so did we. She obviously had overstock, maybe not of the Bead book, but certainly others we'd consigned over the years.

So, within an hour we'd sold $200.00 worth of books, *The Coyote Bead* had gone out of print, and Jo wrote us a check. Then I bought Laura a belated birthday gift of a woven pullover. The old timer at the counter who made that sale said, "Have a look at this Hopi kachina we just got in."

I examined the cottonwood, painted carving. Like all kachinas, it was unusual, and beautiful at the same time. The old timer, who seemed like he'd just popped out of the Appalachian hills, (or maybe Deadwood or Dry Gulch) said what almost seemed like an Al-lan poem. I looked at the man carefully, thinking he might just be Al-lan and then remembered that Al-an only had two guises and this man didn't have fur, nor did he have a faintly blue face. He was old, crochety, white-bearded, barb-humored.

"This here kachina is sight-impaired. Now look at the little bundle on his back. The little short person riding caboose on the big guy is crippled as they come. Therefore, as I see it, the big one's lame, the little one on his back is sighted just fine and together, the way it goes: The blind's being led by the legless. Get it?"

I smiled. "I really get it, and I'll tell you why. My great aunt couldn't walk, she had a thing called 'drop foot'. Her feet wouldn't lay flat the way feet are supposed to. So she was in a wheelchair the entire time I knew her. Now, her husband was blind. She couldn't walk. He couldn't see. Together they were sort of like real-life versions of your kachina."

The old man cackled. "If that don't beat all!" Then he said, while rubbing his white beard, "See no evil walk no evil."

"That's about the size of it. But, by the way, my great aunt lived to be 99 and she would've made it to one hundred, but she told me, 'I've seen it and done it a hundred times already and I don't need to celebrate it. She died that night, one day ahead of her 100th birthday."

The old man's jaw dropped. "If that don't beat all," he said.

***

When we got back to The Veranda, our parrot George was screaming. That happens sometimes when we go away. He likes us where he can keep an eye on us.

You gotta love him, I always say. Well, we do. But you don't.

Having had George since he was a baby (and that was 40 years ago) we do love him. But sometimes, like any bad-behaved two-year-old, George is hard to love. Just as he's hard not to laugh at!

For example. George doesn't like bare feet; he'll attack you if you meet him barefooted.

He's also deadset against nudity. He doesn't see it that way though—when someone's naked George thinks they've lost their feathers. A featherless man, or woman, is not to be trusted in George's book.

He doesn't like men or women with big hair. Especially if their hair is red. That's a cause for attack. We've seen him fly at a woman with big, red, curly hair, and land on her head and start pecking at her. Now, one time this lady friend of ours, who liked to go around naked, came out of the bathroom suddenly. The sun was in her hair and it was bright reddish gold, and she had naked feet, a bare-naked body, and George came at her like a sudden storm.

Our friend was calm and cool and she waited until I unhooked George's claws from her red gold Afro.

Visitors are always asking, "Does your parrot talk?"

I can't begin to tell them what-all George says because he says so much. It's hard for most people to believe that a parrot not only knows the English language but uses it on us as a weapon sometimes. One time he got lost out in the scrub by our house and we looked for him all day with no luck. We went everywhere calling his name. No response. But just before sundown, we called "Georgie, where are you?" And a little voice way out in the Apache Plume bushes said, "Hell-oh."

We ran toward that greeting and found him and when he was perched on my index finger, he looked me in the eye and said, "What took you so long?"

Once he was walking around on the floor and he came up to his best friend, our miniature dachshund. The dog was old and loved to sleep. George bent over and whispered into the dachsy's ear: "I know you can't talk to me now, so I'll save it for later on."

An editor of mine was giving me instructions on the phone on a revision she wanted and George seemed to intuit that I was being given a really tough assignment, and he suddenly started screaming. My editor who had no sense of humor said, "Mr. Andrews, are you hitting your child?"

Another time, George was swearing a blue streak. We were sitting on our porch, the two of us, and a man passing by on the sidewalk thought the uncomplimentary words were aimed at him. "Say that once more he yelled and I'll come up there and wash your mouth out with soap!"

I said, "Hey, man, you're talking to a bird."

"You give me the bird and I'll wash your mouth out, too!"

Our favorite time with George is watching TV. If he likes the movie, he comments on what he's seeing. Once we were watching a murder mystery where this sneaky husband is constantly cheating on his wife and she finally has enough and when he threatens to beat her up as he's done before, he comes at her and she shoots him. Suddenly, George who's been totally focused on this show, started crying like a baby. I said, "George, what's wrong?" George gave me a hard stare and said, "What happened to the man?" It was then we realized that George liked the bad husband and didn't want him to die.

Thinking about our 40 years with George ...

Now you know why we don't think the supernatural is super or natural.

It just is.

As Al-lan is a talking dog and a blue face man.

Chapter Thirty-Three

I sent off the story about the encounter in Will's basement, calling it "Archive in the Cave of Time".

My editor, Cindy, liked it, posted it, and I got some "likes" on Twitter and FB. Cindy wrote and said "We have over 50,000 subscribers and most of them want stories and interviews dealing with subjects that range from Bigfoot to quarks and from science to magic. Your first-person approach to hand trembling, plus time/space, and meetings with miraculous beings, opens up a whole range of ideas I could suggest to you but I'd rather you continue just as you're doing. Keep them coming because we are an online publication and we are bi-monthly. Many writers can't keep up with us, but I have a feeling you can. Go to it. Your check btw isn't in the mail; we send them out every month electronically. Please send me the bank information on the attached form."

As a matter of habit, I always queried my editors before jumping into something, so as soon as I received her positive feedback, I suggested a story about "bones." Not just any bones, however. Those of a woman lost in time.

When I looked at them, they seemed small and insignificant. The Laboratory of Anthropology in Santa Fe was in the process of carbon dating them. I glanced at the purplish bone flakes on the access table and the larger specimens in the enormous mason jar container and wondered if there was really a story there. In a place like Santa Fe, arguably the oldest city in the U.S., bone fragments and even whole skeletons appeared on a somewhat regular basis.

I wondered what the hook or handle on a feature might be.

To begin with, the story, if it is such, began in a bathroom in the Gambol Building on Johnson Street. The floor had fallen in and a plumbing crew was working at reconstruction of floor, pipes, and, lo and behold, down below the rotted tongue-and-groove flooring there was a bone-spare body … of bone spare bone parts. The plumbers thought little of it. They called the Lab out on

Museum Drive. A white government van came and a couple of archaeologists removed the bones, saying they belonged to a dog or wolf.

Even before I heard about this through the grapevine, the remains were run through a chemical bath and some of the bones were sawed up and put under an ultraviolet microscope and … by the time I got there, there was an angry medicine man from Santa Clara Pueblo saying there was going to be a big lawsuit. And, just like that, the bones were taken away for ceremonial reburial at the Pueblo.

But, by then, I had already trembled them.

I remember how quickly it happened.

The electro-empathetic circuity in my left hand reacted violently to the remains. I pulled my hand away. Too late. I was already in.

Feathery fronds of salt cedar, wind rushed, touched my face.

A pair of hands met mine.

Our bodies entwined.

Standing, I felt the warmth of her skin.

In the bee loud glade, there was no sound except the wind and the humming.

She led me to the cool green of a desert pond.

The bees were everywhere—in the water as well as the air. Some were caught in her blue-black hair which now floated around her shoulder.

She drew me into the mild ripple of sun-warm water. Under my feet I felt cold clay. Her hand pressed, palm open, against my chest. Slowly, ever so gently, she drew me in a dance-like rotation. Around and around.

She was smiling.

Then, quite surprisingly, she pulled me under. I went willingly, my skin against her dark sleek body. She turned and rolled like a river otter, her right hand extending upward, as we prepared to rise and breathe.

No sooner had we reached the surface than a huge hand grabbed her hair and dragged her out of the pond. A giant of a man, clay gray, and with hair hanging in vines, so it seemed, all the way to his knees, had a hold of the water woman. I got out of the water as quickly as I could, not minding that I was without any cover, naked and cold skinned. Shivering, I ran after the whimpering woman and the giant grayish man.

Shortly, he came to a thrown-together cedar hogan.

It seemed normal that I was not running on two legs but rather following behind them on all fours. Doing so, I ran into an old and familiar face—the creased, bead-flecked, red and black visage of Old Man Gila Monster. I was so close to his face, I could feel his breath of old roots and decayed matter from under leaves. He smelled terrible. But I thought fast, and trembled him.

The sandy earth rumbled. My hands, both of them, turned to fingered claws. My eyes were vast portals, glazed with pollen.

I felt a tremendous surge pass through me.

My body shuddered and shook.

My arms and legs shrunk, twisted violently.

I looked at them and they were inscribed with black in tattoos. Dark three-pointed stars covered every inch of me. The thick tail in back of me thrashed in the elm leaf cover. I felt of myself; I was all beaded leather and star inscriptions. Dark stars, the ones that kill. Each finger had lightning in yellow, etched and arrow-pointed.

I was Gila Monster.

My tongue tasted of salt and blood, insect pulp and rotted rabbit.

I entered the gray man's lodge

The giant was waiting for me. He clubbed me with a stone hammer.

I rolled on my back. This is it, I said to myself: I am dead.

But there was life, some kind of life, yet in me and I saw my ribs, backbone and tailbone fly to the twelve winds, and all the while, the giant laughed his large discordant, gravelly laugh.

I felt my vitals disperse like dry autumn leaves.

I trembled myself.

I commanded my parts to return in a whirlwind. My eyes burned and glowed, and I spun in a circle in the dust of the gray man's lodge. There came then a sudden rain of hard dry corn of all colors—white, yellow, blue and red. And with the corn rain came thousands of newly hatched grasshoppers and an equal number of corn-carrying beetles. I chanted the song of lightning struck parts.

Through the tips of my fingers flashes of zigzag fire. This force grew within and without me, and I stood up and was tall, as tall as the gray man. I took his axe from the dirt, and as I put my hands on it, he encircled it with his, so that we grappled over who might wield it.

But when I trembled the axe handle and commanded it to turn to woven horse hair, the gray giant stepped backward in astonishment. The axe handle did as I wished, it swung forward and back. But when it touched my own body it stopped, drew forth greater power and then, lightning-like, soared out of my hands and cut his horrified face in two. The two halves dropped upon his shoulders and he dropped to the floor of his hogan. No blood came from his split head, but instead fountains of butterflies flew out of the cavity of his skull and filled the small, dark chamber.

I carried the naked woman out of the hogan and brought her back to the pond. I noticed that she had a corn-colored butterfly on either eyelid.

Night came. I sang the Great Star Chant and she was cleansed and beautified nine times. The pond water sang with starlight. And the dark stars on my beadwork skin faded in the dawn.

And thus I turned myself back into a man and she went back to being a water goddess, and we each went our separate ways through the centuries.

Chapter Thirty-Four

I was recovering from my last trembling—and believe me when I say recovering. For it takes time to—no other way to put it—to come back to earth. Or to sit squarely, or roundly, in your own skin.

Sitting in the backyard, I watched a mad team of bicyclers, maybe a hundred of them, pumping along lightly with their synchronized audio devices playing a Beethoven symphony. It's the turn of the last century again. On the other hand, it's the future. It's anything but the present and that's the problem. They were all a bunch of hydra-infused underwater blinking reef creatures. In a synchrony of sound and a cacophony of red, blue, white blinking, rotating pinpoint light.

The leaves were beginning to turn and last evening, hiking along the river, I saw a patch of snow through the rain, way up high in the mountains, one large, fat scrap of snow. I saw it gleaming through the spears of silver rain.

Now, the stars were coming out.

I had a flashback to the UFO in Sapello. It seemed so normal to us then; we called it a meteor. Nothing more, nor less, than a glare across the blue heavens. A streak of evanescence. But while it exhilarated us at first, it made for some very rough patches, later on, as I described. The un-sequenced time factor. The juxtaposition of things happening, then happening again. The mind caught in the middle. A miggle and a muggle, my friend Mackie used to say in Jamaica.

I was in that miggle, now, when I saw the burny flare of blue light. It passed poetically and quietly over Franklin Street, tangled in the streetlight brightness of someone's sodium roof-lamp. I had to ask myself—What is it? One of those things again?

It hovered over the adobe garage, was lost again in the density of elms, came out the other side, arcing over Jose's junkyard, and then sloped downward. It fit Etienne's long-ago description of— "the thing that is ineluctable, ineradicable, undefinable, and, always, precisely what it is, a UFO."

"They're erratic," he said, "Satellites aren't."

I followed the thing—it was moving very slowly now—down Franklin to Agua Fria, then down toward the riverside of Urioste, into the expanse of golden-sugared, chamisa bushes. I was jogging along the bike trail there, listening to the river pounding piano chords, when the beam of radiant light, so intense I had to shade my eyes, sort of crash-landed, quiet as a mouse and about the same size, right at my feet. It skidded to a stop, twirled, came off the ground, hovered a few feet in the air, hummed away, burning like a little sun, then … nothing.

The stillness of dreaming cottonwoods. The notes of gliding riversong.

Then it returned.

A bright slice of iridescent light. The kind you see in a solar eclipse. Too harsh to focus on and clearly see. Yet too stunning not to try to see.

Then darkness swallowed it up again and I jogged up to it.

For some reason I reached down and touched it.

And jerked my hand back.

A funny sounding, little voice said, "Don't touch the hull, pal."

Now that line I remembered from Dr Frey the night he was abducted, taken to Manhattan from White Sands in what (he later clarified) was a mere matter of seconds, human-time.

I smelled something like burnt ozone and frozen smoke.

Then one side of the black object raised up. There was a tiny man inside at the wheel—but there was no wheel. He leaned toward me. Despite his mousey appearance I recognized Al-lan.

"Get in," he said.

"I'm too big," I said.

He laughed, high and squeaky. "Tremble down, bud."

I tried. But I couldn't seem to get it up.

"Sorry," I said. I looked over my shoulder. Beethoven's bicycle warriors were returning. They were about 100 yards away.

"Get in," Al-lan said.

And there he was standing next to me wearing a pulled-down Australian sheep-herder's hat, his face blue as gorgonzola cheese.

The bikers were 50 yards away.

"Give me your hand," Al-lan said.

I did this. His hand covered mine.

"Now tremble," he ordered in a whispery voice.

I tried again, willing the action from deep within.

Nothing happened.

My stomach tightened.

The cotillion of bikers was 25 yards away.

"Relax," Al-lan whispered. "Where do you see yourself?"

"In a bad place," I told him.

"See yourself swimming in a champagne glass."

The bikers were less than fifteen feet away.

They started shouting: "Coming up on your left. Coming on your right. Coming forward. Get the hell out of the way."

I trembled.

We were in the tiny conveyance. It was like a miniature smart car. Very miniature. By the time the bikes were on us and we heard their thunder and Beethoven noise and the river roaring all at the same time, we were aloft and then nothing but a beam of laser light weaving in between the stars, stitching them up and shafting hither and yon, going faster than the speed of light, or so it seemed to me, but at the same time, we seemed to be standing still and not moving at all.

I somehow managed to speak. I could see Al-lan was enjoying this, all of it. The suddenness. The tranquility. The absurdity. He took off his hat and put it on his right knee. "Welcome to the real world," he said. Then he corrected it: "That is, the r-e-e-l world. All light! Look, Ma, no hands."

I was feeling, at that time, a little sick to my stomach.

He seemed to understand.

"You feel as if there's no gravity. But there is, my friend. You just can't really feel the way you did on earth. This is like starlight compelled to move by the power of Dark Matter. Do you understand?"

I shook my head. Here I was in a tiny container shooting through galactic space, and he was asking me to comprehend the incomprehensible.

"I could give you an algebraic equation."

"Go ahead, I won't understand it."

The heavenly lights meanwhile streaked by us like ghostly filaments imbued with brilliance. Or perhaps more like the streaking rain on the windshield of a car. Yet the car, as it were, that we were in was without walls. We were seated, talking, in the empty space of the continuum.

"This is gravity at a distance," Al-lan explained reasonably. "This star car's powered by Dark Matter that you can't touch, see or feel, that you can't even know, really. It's nothing more than a warp in the fabric of space and time."

Constellations whizzed by us.

"Are we under the Santa Fe River?" I asked.

"Might as well be," he answered. "It's all the same. It's energy versus space, time and gravity."

A thousand Milky Ways slurped past us.

Moons upon moons orbited by.

Clusters of stars, beehives jamming for all they were worth, came and went, clustered and mustered and blew by, and yet more and more came upon their escape into infinity.

"Are you missing mass yet?" Al-lan asked.

He glanced at my confused face. "I mean, of course, are you missing the mass of matter to which, as a person born human, you've been umbilically attached, since the beginning?"

"Since the beginning of my life?"

He smiled. "Yes, that too. But rather the beginning of galactic time. The magellanic gases, the lumen-power up here is extraordinary to a human being. Let me tell you, you'll have more tremble-energy down below that you can ever imagine. After this, you'll be the destroyer of worlds. That is to say, worlds of mind. There will be no orbital staying channel for you. You'll be, in short, unpowered by gravity as you know it, or as expressed in the many books on astrophysical dimensions. You'll be a sort of free agent in the nexus of astral dark matter. The under-luminous, non-luminous will not exist for you. All that is in the past for you now. You will be like a bicycle rider in a star cluster of purest energy. Past, present and future will present themselves as one word, pastpresentfuture. The nuclear alphabet of human potentials will disintegrate at the blink of an eye."

I could think of only one thing to say … "Why me?"

Chapter Thirty-Five

I got my answer at 4 AM the following morning.

"Bonjour," came the soft voice from the past. "Jacques?"

No one but Etienne called me that. "Certainment. C'est vous, Etienne."

"Tout comme ca. C'est moi, veritable!"

"Je ne surprise pas, mon ami. Apres le movement de machine celestial de Al-lan."

He chuckled. "All right," he said, "Vous parlez un petite peu Francais."

"Tres petite peu, Etienne."

"I heard the news," he said, switching to English. "First I felt it. Then I visioned it. Then I got a Messenger alert from Al-lan himself and he told me you'd had the first-class ride of your life in his ... what did he call it?"

"His Dark-Matter-Of-Fact-Machine."

"It sounds better en Francais, mon ami."

I flashed back to when I last heard from Etienne. Was it possible we hadn't spoken since 1980? That had to be right, when my articles came out on Dr Frey and our visit to White Sands. Yes, almost thirty years ago.

"Are you still a UFOlogist?" I asked.

There was a hesitation, as he said something in French to someone. I could tell he was in a Parisian café. "Espresso noir pas de sucre."

"That's the way I like it," I said.

"So ... the reason I called, old friend of the firmament, was to find out if you knew anything about the mouse invasion."

"I'm not sure I—"

"—You do know what I'm talking about ..."

"Al-lan doesn't share that many secrets with me."

Etienne said, "Hmmm."

I could hear him sipping his coffee. Then he lit a cigarette and I imagined the cloud of thick blue Gauloises smoke spreading across the table.

"Still smoking, Etienne?"

"I tried to quit, mon frere. But—"

"—You liked smoking better."

He said nothing, then: "Al-lan tells me everything. But he never takes me up in that Ma-chine magnifique. Maybe one day. I think he thinks I want to go more than anything in the world."

"Isn't that true?"

He chuckled under his breath. "C'est ne pas vrai."

"You've outgrown your fantasy of being abducted then?"

"Oh, that ended long ago. I had a bad time with one right after I was deported. That was just after I saw you for the last time. They took me, and experimented with me. Operated on me. Took parts out, put parts in. Then, after returning me to our little globe, they periodically returned and gave me check-ups. I have nothing to complain about except for one thing."

"—And that is?"

"I haven't aged an hour since we last saw each other. I'm sad to say, I look exactly the same as when you and I were with Dr Frey."

"You're telling me that's a bad thing?"

"—And I haven't had a common cold since then either. Not a single sniffle. Not a wrinkle crept across my face. And I have the sex drive of a thirteen-year-old."

I shook my head and sighed. "That bad, huh?"

"Worse. I can tell you this: My friends are in their seventies now and they are beginning to die off. They see me and they turn away. I look too young to be in their league and they feel it and give me the cold shoulder. To the youngest, I look different. I don't look like them. They seem to smell my distance from them. It's an animal thing, I suppose. My DNA has been altered and others sense that and stay away from me. I'm lonely here on planet earth, Jacques, and I can't go up into the stars either. They, too, have rejected me. Maybe their experiment didn't work. I don't know. All I know is, I'm all alone, except for Al-lan, and did I tell you, he's crazy?"

"He's an extraterrestrial, not a nut case."

"No, you have that wrong. He's both. Right now he's obsessed with some space character named Nom-de-Plume or some such. He says you know him, as well. So, from what he says, that guy is from a Dark Matter planet that has few survivors at present. They are humanoids, I believe, or anyway, they look like them. But they have two missions in life, Al-lan says. They want to re-populate this planet with those of their kind and they have devised a clever way of doing so. Almost totally non-violent. Nothing at all like a take-over, as you might say. More like a take-into."

"You're not making very much sense, Etienne."

"Neither was Al-lan. But his authorization, you know, from Xerxes, is to exterminate these other extraterrestrials from Orgone."

"From Oregon?"

"I think Al-lan said Or-gone. At any rate, he, Al-lan, has been annihilating these life forms, one at a time. He says it's getting pretty old, doing this, and he wants to retire. But he's got to get this Plume man and his freak family first."

"Do you mean Appleplum?"

"Oui. Pomme-de-terre-plume-Smith, he said, The guy's a sex maniac with martial arts powers you wouldn't believe, according to Al-lan."

I guffawed into the phone. "I've dealt personally with those powers—they're formidable."

Etienne drew hard on his cigarette and I heard him exhale for a good little while. His coffee cup rattled. "What is your email address?" he asked.

I told him. "Give me a moment and I'll contact you that way. In the mean-time, Blessings, old compatriot. By the way, have you aged … normally, shall we say?"

"I have plenty of grey hairs, if that's what you mean."

"You're lucky, Jacques. Very lucky."

I laughed and shook my head. "Aging isn't a matter of luck, it's a matter of longevity, and then … poof, you're gone, like that ciggy-boo you just smoked."

"No," he said sadly. "It is the greatest blessing. We think the opposite. We imagine health is the answer to all life's problems. It isn't. Good health is a curse. It's a pox. Maybe, however, bacterium yersinia pestis is the final so-lution, I don't know … but I hope so. Au revoir, frere de guerre!"

He hung up abruptly.

Shortly after, a message tumbled into my Kindle.

Etienne had written:

"Bacterium yersinia pestis has been with humanity for a very long time. It comes from flea bites from infected rodents, primarily mice and rabbits. The disease has the pneumonic component, too. But it can be bubonic as well as pneumonic. Jacques, we are talking here of what we used to call the plague. BTW, "rabbit fever", so-called is another thing and it is called tularemia. But as far as the other, the bacterium yersinia pestis, it easily infects dogs. Al-lan has been risking his life trying to deal with this beginning epidemic. You know, he plays "switchbitch" with dogs as a disguise when he comes down here, and I think he may have contracted the plague as a result. For all we know, he could be dying right now, blessed crazy soul, and what a nice way to go, I might add. You won't see me on any IVs if I get the rodent pestis, I'll tell you that. And if you haven't found that life is one boring repetition after another, let me tell you, it will happen sooner or later, and then you'll be just like me. Al-lan hung up on me when I told him that, which is why I'm messaging you on email, so you won't be angry with me. At this point I don't care if the Orgonians, what's left of them, unleash their mice legions and kill us off. Human beings will do that efficiently, as we have seen, through the bullet, the ballet, the gun, or the bomb. That's about all I have to say. Tout amour, vieux ami."

Chapter Thirty-Six

When I thought about Etienne and our explorative inquiries into UFOlogy, our travels all over New Mexico, it brought back his wonderful wife, Mina. If he was the peanut butter in the P&J, Mina was the jam.

But mainly on books. Over the years since his deportation two things had grown large in her life—her work as a book designer and her passion for food. She'd become a gourmand, and a well-nigh famous one with a syndicated column. In the course of reviewing the foodie scene in New Mexico, Mina, minus Etienne had become jocular and round. Then she surprised everyone by suddenly dying.

When Laura and I first heard the news of her passing we were at the Miami Book Fair International and I was in the storytelling tent reading from my latest children's book. I remember bursting into tears. I had in my book bag one of the recent books Mina had designed. It was called *Floating Stone*, the selected translations of the great Zen poet Miyazawa Kenji. This was, in fact, the launch for the book, and now our dear friend, Mina, was gone.

I wondered how Etienne was taking it. He couldn't return to the U.S. for the funeral because he'd been deported. His deportation was instigated by the federal criminal offense of performing psychic healing with a Filipino surgeon who was on an FBI wanted list. A sad situation.

Mina always loved humor. She and Laura and I used to tell funny stories and share jokes and laugh until our sides ached. I wondered how hard she might've laughed at seeing me on stage when the boy in the front row asked me if I could "do" Donald Duck.

That is a tiger trap invented by kids to foil traveling performers. There is always one thing you can't, and shouldn't, do unless of course you are a voice-over master, which I am not. Yes, I fell into the trap and did a pretty poor D Duck, and the kid shouted, "Your Donald Duck SUCKS!"

I could hear Mina's laugh bursting from a heavenly cloud.

I felt somehow that Mina would've also pushed me back into that dead-house. She would've had a lot of questions about it. Where were the bodies you thought you saw? Where did all the mice go to? What about the "Lucky Ducky" note from Appleplum? Was all that stuff just a hallucination? She was better at detection and "logique" than her husband. She was really good at measurements and calibrations.

So I went back to the deadhouse and sniffed around.

In the half-light I saw corpses, stacked floor to ceiling as before, like cords of wood. And all around were mice, nibbling at the dead skin of the dead. When they saw me they turned and came at me in a brown, ripply wave. I danced to higher ground—a wooden box which collapsed, but I'd already trembled into the pigeon roost in the rafters. I was pigeon for a second or two before I trembled out of there and into a feral cat on a fence post outside. From the cat whose belly was growling, or else it was the additional me in her gut and brain that made the growl, but I was gone by then into the body of a homeless man sleeping by the prairie dog village. I shifted quickly out of his nimbus cloud of body odor into a Victorian-paunched, paterfamilias prairie dog and from there, I—this even stretched my imagination—into Laura.

There she was standing pretty in the wind, and I dropped in, and she whispered, "Oh," which was what she used to say when we had sex when we were barely out of our teens.

Being in Laura was interesting … then, and now, as a bodily guest, so to speak. Her shoulder ached and she felt tired, but her mind was, as always, swift as a running stream. I trembled her more, and flipped back many years to when we were truly teens and I first saw her naked in a bathtub. Being a redhead, to me, she was extraordinarily beautiful. A redhead naked in a white tub is something altogether memorable. I retrieved a mental snapshot of that memory and trembled off into George sitting on the cagetop in our kitchen.

George was edgy—to say the least. He started hollering and then flew into the wall mirror. I suppose there's no explanation except that my drop-ins were gradually becoming less gradual. I was popping in kind of hard and sudden. I would have to sort of meditate my way into animate life forms.

Actually, I'd never tried to drop into myself because "myself" wasn't there. But now I saw a photograph of me on the fridge, a recent one, and as George (me) was staggering around on the floor, I hopped back into myself, and in that instant became myself.

Exhaustion overtook me and I took myself to bed.

And that is where Laura found me.

She wanted something, that, despite being a little worn around the edges, I was only too glad to give.

Chapter Thirty-Seven

There are three kinds of diviners in the Navajo tribe. Two of them are now mostly gone. But even the word "diviner" is gone as well, mainly because it was never used by tribal people. Anthropologists used it, not Indians. There's no word for it in Navajo but they do say, "That which he knows" — something intrinsic felt by the practitioner (another word not used by Navajos).

The diviner, practitioner, mystic gathers information from somewhere beyond the five senses. That which he knows might also be: That which comes to him. But not necessarily outside himself. Which is to say, other people do not necessarily hear it.

Listeners may pray for listening to come.

And when it does it may be in the form of a bear's cough, a rattler's buzz, or distant thunder. It might also come in the form of a crying sound. If so, the patient, the sick one who is being "listened" may be on the threshold of death. Crying is not a good sound nor is the stargazer's vision of a horse's teeth being pulled. Could that be a sound as well? Possibly so.

All of these things are hard to talk about. It's a lot easier to say that there are four basic kinds of practitioners in the tribe: Listeners, stargazers and sungazers, and of course, tremblers.

The reason I am thinking about diviners ...

I met one the other day. A boy. About ten years old. I was visiting a school, giving an author's presentation. After my talk kids gathered in the auditorium to buy my book, *The Coyote Bead*, the story of the Long Walk of the Navajo.

I signed fifteen books and was packing to leave when the boy appeared before me. He had waited for the others to leave.

"I want a book," he said.

Oddly enough, this ten-year-old looked like a very old man. This happens, and you see it in schools, and it's rarely a medical condition. Sometimes it's a performance, so to say. Other times it's a condition brought on by an unusual living experience. Whether it was an unconscious act or a medically diagnosed situation, the boy himself stood before me and demanded a book.

"Do you have a parental signature on the school's book form?" I asked. That was how the books were distributed—librarian/parent/principal signed and then the kids got the book and no money was exchanged. The billing came later from the school, direct to parent.

The boy looked me in the eye and said, "I have no book form. But I want a book."

He continued to stare at me. It was an unrelenting stare. Not that of a boy. More like a wizened and perhaps a disgruntled old man.

He glared.

"I am supposed to give books only with signed permissions."

"The hell with that," the boy said. His eye burned into mine. Suddenly I remembered where I'd seen such an eye—while hand trembling into Gila Monster. It was the Gila Monster eye, all right. Somehow the boy had it.

"Look," I said, you ..." But I didn't finish. The boy's left hand was shaking slightly. His fingers trembled. They were pointed at me. I felt an unusual warm vibration around my upper chest.

The boy was in.

I said, "Oh," and remembered Laura.

Then I gave the boy the book. "I hope you like it," I said, recovering myself, as he vacated me.

He never said thank you. He said nothing. He left the auditorium.

I found myself tired and cold and a little bewildered.

I'd never been trembled by another.

I did remember though when I was eleven or twelve being in the closet, trembling. And once something came over me like a hot blanket, and I started to sweat. I had to get out of the closet. I did. And there in front of me was a small white buffalo. A calf.

The little gentle creature stayed with me for about a year. When it left I cried and cried. I missed it so badly I ached all over. But it never came back. It was gone for good, I supposed, and I finally accepted this. Once I was a teenager, the trembling in the closet took on a new turn. It got me, in fact, out of the closet more often than it got me in. I began doing daredevil stunts to test the tremble, and to see if I was, as I suspected, immortal.

Before leaving the school, I checked in with the principal.

"There was a boy who sort of demanded a book, so I gave it to him. He had no book form, and he was a little bit strange, I thought, but maybe just nervous."

The principal chuckled. "You met Randall Allworthy," he said with assurance.

"Is he … all there … I mean, he seemed a bit odd, cold, strange, whatever you want to call it."

"He's not autistic," the principal said. "If that's what you're getting at. He simply lives with his grandfather, and has become an exact duplicate of the old man who's eighty-something. The kid's got the old man's shake, too. He dresses conservative, even for this school. I'm pretty sure the old man buys Randall's clothes and has taught him, by proxy, as I would say, how to be, well, an old geezer." The principal laughed. "It's not really funny, you understand. But we deal with it every day and sometimes, well, sometimes … you know."

"I think I do."

"One thing, though, the old man won't pay for books. Doesn't think the boy needs them. If you think old school, I think the old coot's ancient school. He believes schools are a bunch of nonsense. A boy should learn to be by himself, the old man once told me right here in this office where you're standing."

"Has he gotten any medical diagnosis," I questioned.

"Grandpa won't sign for it. The kid's a kind of maverick old timer in the midst of a fast-moving generation of device clickers. This boy Randall has probably never seen or heard of a portable radio, let alone a hand-held cellphone. You do the best you can, is all I can tell you, and the boy's doing the best he can, I can tell you that. He's got a rough row to hoe. You know, I didn't mention it, but the boy's parents ran off and abandoned him. We had him in the hospital on an IV before we discovered he had a grandfather."

"Now he's become a grandfather."

"You got that right. Blessings for giving him the book. Maybe it'll do something for him."

"There are some schools on the reservation that have benefited from it."

The principal smiled. "I did," he said. "I read all the books that come in, believe me. What made yours different was that you told the story from the point of view of the Indians who refused to go on The Long Walk. The ones who stayed in the canyons and ate rabbits and small game and somehow survived those years. But I had to admire their cussedness, their refusal. They stayed. Their peach trees were chopped and burned, their lives were shattered like their corn crops and yet they hung on. Didn't you say in there somewhere that the Navajos are the largest indigenous tribe in the U.S? How did a guy like you get in with them anyway?"

I laughed at the way he put it. "A guy like me, around fifty years ago, went to school with them. The same way Tony Hillerman told me he did. My dad used to say, referring to the way he learned things, 'Even with a fool something rubs off.' In my case a small circle of Navajo friends saved my life, and I've never forgotten."

"I'd really like to hear about that sometime," he said. "Maybe when you come back for another visit. Right now I have a teacher's meeting to conduct. Thank you for coming to Brook Elementary, and especially, for treating Randall the way you did."

We shook hands.

Driving out of the parking lot, I got a tingle in my left hand.

I wondered if Randall did, too.

Chapter Thirty-Eight

A few days later, I got the following email.

> Jack,
> I liked what you said in your book.
> Is it true?
> Randall

***

> Randall,
> It's certainly true if you believe it's true.
> If you don't believe it's true, no amount of proof
> is going to make it true."
> Jack

***

A week later, another email.

> Jack,
> If you put a blue bead into one coyote pup's mouth
> And a white bead in another coyote pup's mouth,
> do you get magic strong enough to kill a bad guy like TwoFace?
> Randall

***

Randall,
The Navajo medicine man who told that story
believed it to be true. He said it, his son told it to me,
I wrote it.
Jack

***

Jack,
You wrote it, I believe it. Sort of.
But tell me, have you ever written a book about shoes?
Randall

***

Randall,
I am going to write one just for you ….
Jack

***

I let it steep for a while.

Shoes …

I forgot about it in the press of the Wyrd assignments, which were taking up more and more of my time and paying more and more of my bills.

Then one day, remembering Randall, I wrote The Great Shoe Book especially for Randall.

What inspired it was the large number of cheerless, hopeful, washed-up, just starting-out, wide eyed, closed eyed, pinched face, happy-sad homeless people in and around Santa Fe. I saw them every day in every unlikely, and likely, place you can imagine. Down by the railyard, at Dunkin on St Francis, on Alameda by the river, by the closed down liquor store named Carol's Bottles, on virtually every corner with a median where someone could hang with a sign and a frown or a bigger than life smile. And no matter how smudged of face and beat their clothing might be, they all had a curious charm, at least to me, and a purposeful angle, as well.

There was the woman whose sign read: *Homeless, Hungry, Pregnant.*

The man whose sign said: *Thank you, anyway.*

The smiling Buddha-face guy who held up a banner of beautiful script: *Your dollar will last me one week.*

I saw an old man give the Buddhistic dollar seeker several handfuls of cash. This equally smiley old philanthropist just stopped his car by the side of the road, and started stuffing money in the panhandler's pockets.

The whole voyald, as William Saroyan said.

Anyway—here's the little book I wrote for Randall:

THE GREAT SHOE BOOK

> People who shine their shoes
> People who wear no shoes
> People who smile
> People who cannot smile
> People who do not believe but know
> People who are poor-ly understood
> People who are richly-deserving
> People who have hope because they are hope-less
> People who did not come because they are frightened
> People who are frightened because they did not come
> People who live on the road
> People who cannot get on the road
> People who float
> People who sink
> People who can be counted on
> People who cannot be counted
> People who give their best
> People who best serve others
> People who try
> People who are just trying
> People who wish
> People who wish they had a wish
> People who ascend
> People who descend
> People who are there
> People that aren't there
> People that never were there

People, yes, people
Purple people
Popular people
Broke people
Brick people
Stricken people
Strucken people
Tall people
Shrunken people
Pronounceable people
Unpronounceable people
People of all perplexions
People of all complexions
People of all persuasions
People of all ideations & nations
People of the people-less oceans
   Of people-less-ness.

***

I sent it off to Randall. Two days later, he wrote back:

Jack,
 I think the book should be called *People.*
Randall

***

I thought about this.

Then I remembered what a bestselling author said to me:

"A writer is a person with a reader."

Chapter Thirty-Nine

The fourth and final time I entered the deadhouse, I dropped into a trap.

The red dust floor went uphill at one point, and for the first time, I went up and walked on it.

It was covered with mouse tracks.

I bent down to look at them and the floor caved.

I fell, and fell, pummeled by falling dirt and stones.

I dropped into absolute night.

And suddenly came to a stop in soft granular sand like a damp riverbed, waterless but nonetheless wet. I was sitting rather than standing and the shock of the landing made my spine ache all the way from backbone to skull.

I passed out and when I awoke, I saw light winking at me from a juncture in the stone cave that I'd fallen into. When I looked upwards, hoping to see the red dirt hole I'd fallen into, I saw only black. The walls of the passageway were smooth and cold.

What had I gotten myself into?

A tiny mouse squeaked at my feet.

I trembled into him and found myself running into sunlight.

I was out of the tunnel, but where?

I blinked in the harsh light of day, the hot sun on my head, cold sand underfoot. Four foot. I had tiny pink hands with little claws. I could see every seam in the stones, close-up. It was as if my night-shaped eyes were rapidly adjusting to the day bright desert. I could see tiny glittery mica rocks, and the smells I smelled were heavenly plants and herbs, trees and bushes.

Then, right in front of my eyes, I saw a beautiful woman giving birth. She was on a bed of reddish-brown clay. She birthed a baby.

I stood on my hind feet, amazed.

And watched.

A small marsh wren came down out of the blue sky and cut the navel cord with its beak. It bathed the first baby in sky and spring water. Then it was wrapped in darkness.

The second baby came. Wren dried it and titmouse cut the cord. Then marsh wren bathed this baby in morning dew.

How I knew this, I couldn't say, but somehow I knew that this second baby was Tobachischin, Born of Water.

The first baby was a bit bigger and it was dried, cord-cut, and bathed similarly as Born of Water. But it was wrapped, as I watched, in a blanket made of dawn. This baby was named Nayenezgani, Monster Slayer.

Their mother, as I came to know, was White Shell Woman or Etsan-ah-Tlehay. And it was she who asked wren and titmouse to dig a pit. She then placed her babies into it and covered it with stones.

This was done so that Gray Monster, Yeitso Lapai, would not come and eat the newborns. You could hear his heavy footsteps as he searched for warm birthed flesh. Babies were best, he thought, but he would eat any two-legged person because two-leggeds are said to be good to eat.

All this I knew. But, as for me, little mouse, I ate only seeds.

I was hungry now and went searching for seeds, nuts, and sweet pollens.

I found these and ate plentifully and the dust of golden pollen was on my fur.

When I returned to the newborn boys and their mother, four days had passed. I knew this because the boys were beginning to be well-grown.

All the same, danger was afoot, and I could feel it coming.

There were tracks all around the pit and it happened that Yeitso the Gray saw them and smelled them and came to the place where the children were hiding with their mother.

"What is this I smell?" the monster said.

"It is nothing," the mother answered.

"No, it is something." Yeitso the Gray sniffed the air and the earth. He was very large, fanged and clawed, and terribly ugly with patches of hanging ragged fur where fur should not grow and bare gray skin where fur should grow to hide certain body parts.

He was down now on all fours, sniffing and snorting. Long white strands of drool formed and flowed at the corners of his mouth full of jagged yellow teeth.

"What are these tracks?" Yeitso bellowed. "You are hiding something from me."

"It is not true," White Shell Woman said quickly. "What you see are my knuckle prints in the sand."

He sniffed and drooled, sensing this was a lie.

"I desire children so much but so far I have not been able to have any. But those knuckle prints I made, they are supposed to draw a child to me. It is our way."

"Does that work?" Yeitso asked, dumbfounded by the logic.

"You must make the prints and pray often and then it will work."

"I see," Yeitso said, rubbing his hairy chin. "I will tell my wife and see what she says."

"Have you no children of your own?" White Shell Woman asked.

"One can never have enough children," he replied.

All this I heard clearly and well, for my ears are quite large and they capture almost everything that comes near. But what I couldn't hear, I could see. I saw the boys grow rapidly; in eight days they were big, almost grown to full. But, like boys anywhere, they were very mischievous and disrespectful. They had bows of flash lightning and arrows of crooked lightning.

During the day they prowled about like hunters, drawing their bows and shooting their arrows at feathered birds who had befriended them and who had helped them be born. They had little sense and even when the birds reminded them that they were their friends and family, the boys still sent arrows their way. When not doing that, the boys wrestled in sand and mud and made a terrible mess of themselves. But their mother said nothing because clay on skin is a good thing and will cover the smell of a two-legged person. Yeitso, if he came back, wouldn't be able to sniff out the boys.

The ninth day after their birth, each one asked his mother, "Who is our father?"

She told them, "Your father was cactus tree and prickly pear cactus and that is why your hair is dirty and drippy with oil, and why I have to wash it so often."

The boys did not like having their hair scrubbed of oil, but they did like making fun of each other, and they would taunt one another by saying: "Your hair is filth, mine is clean." And the other would answer, "It is just the opposite, my hair is shiny and beautiful while yours is ratty and dirty."

By the tenth day after their birth, I had gone to get more seeds.

When I came back to the pit, they were gone.

Chapter Forty

I nibbled seeds and watched.

The boys were growing more fearless.

But I heard their mother say to them, "You would like to know your father but it may not be possible. He has many guardians, watchers who protect him."

She knew that, more than anything, they wanted to see their father. Merely to set eyes upon him. But if that could not be …

I saw them now, and for some days after, speaking secretly the way boys do. Talking softly as boys want to do when they have plans.

Their mother, knowing the ways of boys somehow, gave each one a medicine bundle of white shell and one parrot feather for each.

That night, as I made my little bed of straws and scattered fibers that I found, I heard the boys talking low.

"She doesn't want us to go to see our father," said the eldest, Nayenezgani.

Tobachischin said, "She is afraid we will be hurt."

"The guardians?"

"They may be enemies to us."

Then Nayenezgani spoke out loud, "I am afraid of no one, and no thing."

"I am not so confident," Tobachischin said.

But then their mother, overhearing them, spoke. "Go to sleep," she said, "Dawn will come more quickly than you would think."

In the morning when I awoke, the boys were gone and I saw their tracks in the sand. Or, rather, their track. For it was a single one.

I followed it in the pre-dawn light.

It was one track into which more than one foot was placed to hide the truth: that two boys were afoot.

I crept closely behind them with my little bundle of sunflower seeds and pine nuts and juniper berries on my back.

The boys went to a small pond which was yellow with cattail pollen, willow pollen and other pollens; and these they put upon their heads so that they were yellow, too.

I scampered into the yucca woven shirt of Tobachischin. He never saw me, as I am lighter than a heron's down feather. There I stayed, snug and sound, while these clever boys rode upon a rainbow. This was a good trick and it worked until a great hill of dark sand fell upon them. It seemed to have a will of its own and it nearly smothered them, and I, as well. Each time the boys aimed the rainbow at the hill, the hill came down on them. Altogether this happened four times.

Nayenezgani laughed. Then he began a rain song, and his brother joined in and the two gestured with their hands and brought down a strong rain, and the rain washed over the hill and cut it down in size until it was just an anthill.

I was glad we were through that, and traveling on without any more trouble. That is, until they came to a large lake with sharp, slicing reeds at the banks. I can swim, so I wasn't afraid; neither were they. But the reeds had a different plan. They danced and sliced in the wind and came at the boys cutting their arms and legs. I got a bad swipe and felt the knife-sharp edge of a reed. I left drops of blood on the shirt fold of Tobachischin. He paid no attention because he had wounds of his own. As did his brother whose face was now blood red from a cut on his forehead.

It was then that I tried a trick of my own.

I trembled myself—me, a little mouse person—into the great black, dangerous reeds, and then, seeing a heron fly by, I trembled into heron, turned back around and flew into the reeds, giving them some of their own medicine. Nothing is more soft and pliant than a heron and I used my feathers to block their blows and their knife thrusts. In no time I tired the reeds and they surrendered.

"How did you do that?" Tobachischin asked his brother.

"I didn't," he answered. "We have a strong ally with us."

"But who?"

"We don't know."

I saw reed rats by the lake then, and I trembled from great heron into reed rat, and then entered into Tobachischin's shirt fold.

"I feel something," he said.

"Don't speak of it now," Nayenezgani replied. He was looking straight ahead. From out of the lake came an endless snake, rippling like the water itself, and coming on with an angry face.

Each time the boys tried to escape the snake, it encircled them, drawing its coils closer and closer until it was almost upon them. The boys then sang the snake song to charm the snake. But its head loomed over us and its fangs were visible and its forked tongue flashed lightning.

Four times the boys sang the snake song.

But by the last verse of the song, the great snake had them in its coils and was preparing to eat them.

I saw only one thing to do. Knowing that snakes like to eat reed rats more than anything else, I danced out of the loose folds of Tobachischin's shirt and offered myself for the giant snake to eat. Straight away he dropped the boys and took after me.

I was having a good run in the opposite direction, away from the great snake. But he was everywhere. His length was as long and round as the earth, and suddenly, before I could do anything, I was scooped up and swallowed by the endless, overpowering snake.

Then I found myself in the dark gurgling river of his body. His ribs were above me, glittering darkly. Below was the noise of his belly and the river carrying many animals like myself, but some I had never seen before. There were many smaller snakes and some rats as large as dogs, not to mention dogs as large as giant rats, and all of these creatures were a moving mass, throbbing mass. Soon all of them were dead, drowned.

I, alone, lived.

But I hadn't long to live.

I wondered how the boys were doing …

But there was no time for wondering.

I was as good as dead, I was so tired.

The belly of great snake was the end for any animal with powers less than the largeness of a snake that could encircle the earth.

Then I chanced to see another living being.

It was field rat woman. She had woven a raft of cedar twigs and she was floating on it.

"May I come on?" I asked.

"Sure," she said. Then, after I climbed onto her raft, she told me: "There is but one way to live in the belly of great snake, and that is to make him sick. First, we must eat to keep up our strength, then we will apply a trick that may work to stop the river of blood we find ourselves in."

I did what she said, and ate what she told me to eat, though it made me sick to do so.

We ate cedar facing east. It was too dark in the cavern of the snake for me to see the directions, but she knew them in spite of the darkness.

We ate, facing south, yucca seeds and cactus buds. These were good foods but I was already stuffed when she said, "Now we must have a dessert of coyote shit." I hesitated but she informed me, "If we don't do this we will never get out of here. Eat!"

I did what she said. Strange to say, the shit of coyote was not so bad because he, coyote, had recently eaten a meal of peaches, so that his dung was peach flavored. I ate all of it.

Then she said, "Last we wash this food down with the vomit of buzzards."

She produced a soft drinking pouch full of such filth I have never seen or smelled. "You must not vomit up the vomit I give you," she explained. "Just do as I do." She then tilted and squeezed the pouch and a stream of buzzard puke flew into her mouth, and she swallowed.

I did as she did. I will not tell what it tasted like, but it was worse than awful. My body shuddered so badly I thought I would die. But she said one last thing: "I will drink once more, then you will finish it off."

Which she did and then she gave me the last and I drained the pouch, and started to heave, but she stopped me, saying, "If you lose one drop to your whiskers, we shall die in snake's belly, and the magic won't work."

I stopped heaving then because I wanted to live.

And even more than that, I wanted to destroy great snake.

And follow the boys wherever they had gone.

With flints then, she struck a light.

The interior of great snake gleamed with curved belly-bones.

Wood rat woman then caught a tiny spark from the flints, blew on it four times, and placed it softly on top of the raft.

She continued to blow as she got off the raft and beckoned me to do the same, which I did.

The river of blood and dead creatures in various forms of rot passed around us and bumped up against us. I saw the empty eye sockets of desert pigs with snouts decayed and falling away from the bone. The shells of locusts lodged in my fur and rattled. Many small snakes and worms sought shelter in my ears. I held on to the raft with all my might as the cedar smoke began to billow and fill the belly chamber of great snake.

In a little while, we could feel the body of him begin to writhe and turn.

He rolled and we rolled with him and all the undigested creatures swept across our faces, but we still held on to the burning, smoking raft.

There was a tremendous upheaval.

A volcano of vomit now came from great snake's fanged mouth and we passed out of it in a flash flood of the dead.

We tumbled and rolled. Free at last, both of us.

I came to understand from wood rat woman that we had been in the belly of great snake for four days and though he was dead, she told me, "They never die until the sundown of the fourth day, which is now, and the sun is just setting, so we must go our separate ways quickly and with no stopping to eat the cactus fruit which is right now so sweet and good."

I did as she said. Limping toward the west.

She went east and I had no time to thank her she moved so fast.

But I did pick one cactus fruit, red and ripe, and just held it toward the east and said, "This is for you, wood rat woman, I will never forget your kindness as long as I live."

Then I heard the rumbling of great snake as he twisted and cracked his tail. Branches and thorns flew in his wake like a storm of violent arrows.

I soon distanced him.

The sun sank.

I said prayers to his leaving.

And then I saw kangaroo rat, the kind with the tufted tail at the very end. The kind with the bright, big eyes that can easily see in the dark. Wood rats of the lakes have less eyesight, so I trembled into this just-awakening, drowsy, fellow. After a moment or two, I moved with undreamed-of speed and bounce in the direction where the boys were seen battling great snake with me.

I was now a mouse with night vision better than owl's.

But could I find the lost tracks of the twins?

Chapter Forty-One

I couldn't have found the boys had it not been for changing bear woman.

It was she who buried her intestines and sang a song about it. But that is for another time. For this time, I heard her sing to the boys, encouraging them on their journey to meet the Sun Father.

"With the power that you have within," she said, "you will meet your father and then you will destroy the monsters that plague the earth. I will help you and here is my song for you:

> I, changing bear woman,
> To the monsters I go
> Swift arrows work loose
> The power from them falls
> The monsters
> To them I go
> Go la, go he
> Follow me
> I will teach you how
> To hide your guts
> So that no enemy may bring harm
> So that your power may increase
> Go la, go he
> The arrows fall at my five-toed foot."

Then I, kangaroo mouse, heard Nayenezgani say,

"I don't see how this silly song will bring us much luck in getting to our father's house."

Tobachischin said, "But we mustn't annoy or make bear woman angry, for she has much power, and she encourages us on our way."

The boys went on upon the dark plain, and I followed close behind.

Soon they met a woman old and bent; this was spider woman who lived in a house of jet. The moment she blew on her small house, I saw it grow bigger. "Enter my house and I will feed you," spider woman said.

Quickly, before the boys disappeared, I leaped boldly into the bearskin vest bear woman had given Tobachischin as a gift. There, I was secreted and warm.

Spider woman's jet house had four rooms.

There was a small shaft of light that came from a smoke hole in the roof. Where this blade of light burned, spider woman held up a white shell. The light from above shone on it and filled the beam of light with pollen. I peeked out of the vest and peered at spider woman who stirred the air and the pollen and added water to it. This turned to mush, and the boys were asked to eat of it. They spooned it into wooden bowls given them by spider woman.

It was then, as the boys were eating, spider woman, who has more than one eye, as you know, caught sight of me. "Such a lovely big-eared mouse person," she said, admiring my large ears, and touching one of them with her hairy hand. "So soft," she said. "You are lucky to have him as your guardian. He has large eyes and larger ears, and can see and hear far into the night."

"This is the first I have seen of him," Tobachischin said as he ate plentifully of the radiant white corn mush.

"He, too, needs to eat of this," spider woman said, and from the air she spooned more mush.

When we were all done eating, she took her turn, eating the gold air in one swallow.

Then it was time for us to take our leave, so we left through the same door through which the boys had entered. After we stepped clear of it, the doorway shrank to a tiny eye hole. We saw the old woman's eyes gleaming out of the jet peep hole. "Goodbye and good luck," she said. Then she added some leave-taking advice.

We couldn't see her body but we could hear her voice, and see her glinting eyes shining like dark jewels.

"Take care," she said, "and remember—your father is very wicked and very powerful, so here, take this little downy feather, as it too has much power, and can help you in a time of need."

Nayenezgani and Tobachischin said, "May you live in harmony" and they turned and went on their way, with me tucked inside the vest snug as could be.

And so the journey into the dawn continued.

It wasn't long before we came to a crossing. There, a small gray bird, told us, "Who passes this way will grow old, for when the wind brushes against my feathers the dust of old age will dust you and you will rapidly age. You will get so old," he warned, "that you will turn to dust yourself … and then where will you be?"

"Then what should we do?" Nayenezgani asked.

"Old yellow will help you," said the gray bird whose name, he told us, was Nuthatch, in case we should have need of him again.

"Why should we have need of death and dust?" Nayenezgani said scornfully.

Nuthatch answered, "There may come such a time."

Nayenezgani snorted in scorn. "We are destined to live forever," he said.

But Nuthatch just laughed. "No one but your father can say that. Still, I will ask old yellow to help you this once so that you may go on your way."

We waited and as the light of dawn spread out like a blanket, Nayenezgani saw something that stood out upon the yellow sand of the desert. It was more yellow than the sand, otherwise it was the same shape and form.

The rising sand spoke, "I am sphynx moth tobacco worm."

I had never seen anything like him before. He was moving along by pulling his body with his neck. There was a horn on his head. Then, suddenly, he changed; he wore a shirt of evening twilight and a loose skirt of new moon.

"Do you want to race?" he asked.

Before Nayenezgani could say yes, which he surely was going to do, Tobachischin replied to his challenge.

"We could not beat you," he said humbly.

Sphinx moth smiled. "You are right about that, young one. So saying, I will give you some advice. "Your father is terrible. He can kill you with his smoke."

With that, the moth turned worm again.

151

Then he spat a blue phlegm out of his mouth.

"This will prevent your father from killing you with his smoke. Hide it in your ear and rub it all over your body just before you meet your father."

The boys said they would do this. After a little while, there came a gentle, female rain and with it, soon after, a rainbow which we rode upon as before. The rainbow neighed and made the sounds that a horse makes, and I knew that while it was a rainbow it was also a four-legged horse.

From the vantage point of the horseback rainbow, we saw what lay below.

It was an enormous body of water. And it thrived and writhed with water monsters of all colors and kinds.

Water beasts of fin and fang, water horses with feet of flint to kill, twisted monsters of white and black and no particular form, glittering fish of great size that spouted water-flame from their nostrils.

"We are much closer to our father now," Tobachischin told his brother.

"How do you know this?"

"These monsters below that follow us as we move across the clouds, they are the children of the sun, our father's pets, no doubt."

"How do you know?" Nayenezgani repeated.

"It is that which I know," Tobachischin said sharply.

"Then what is next, brother?"

"Look ahead of you, brother."

Nayenezgani looked forward and was amazed, as was I.

For there, right before us, shone the blinding, blazing door of the sun.

And before that door that led to the sun himself, there stood a legion of the most dangerous guardians that ever lived.

The brothers bowed heads, and shivered.

I listened, and quivered.

Chapter Forty-Two

The guardians came at us in deadly pairs.

First, two mountain lions with curved tails and ivory teeth.

They came clawed and angry, snarling.

But I knew the sacred, secret name of these two and I whispered it to Tobachischin and he whispered it to his brother who said the name aloud.

Immediately, the tails of the lions straightened and they lay down, paws extended in peace, heads resting on paws, and a purring noise came from them.

The snake guardians appeared next. I saw they had horns on their heads and dripping silver fangs. They rose up fierce and ready to fight. I could not remember their names at first, but the closer they slid, hissing as they came, the better I understood them. "Tell them how pretty the red spots are on their heads," I whispered to Tobachischin. He repeated this to his brother and Nayenezgani complimented the snake guardians, and their hisses were low like water passing between close rocks. "Tell them how pretty their horns are," I whispered to Tobachischin, and he passed this on to his brother. Nayenezgani praised the horns on the snakes' heads and they lowered their heads to the ground.

The bear guardians stood fast and were now prepared to do what the other guardians were not. They growled and gnashed their teeth and rent the air with their claws, and came forward. Lightning licked the sun door and thunder was heard, and the boys moved toward the bear guardians.

"Tell them 'I AM HERE' I said into Tobachischin's ear.

And this time, he spoke the words and instantly the bears lay down and let us pass upon their heads which were as large as great flat stones but soft and furry, and we could hear the bears make small coughing noises deep in their throats as we walked over them. Then we were directly in front of the doors of the sun.

"Who are you?" came a voice, and the doors opened and a small woman stood before us.

Nayenezgani spoke: "We were told our father lived here."

Tobachischin said, "We have come to see him."

The woman went to the north side of the huge hogan of the sun. When she returned she had a dark blanket made of mist. This she threw out before her and it wrapped itself around the boys and myself and we disappeared into its depths and were lost. But we could still hear the woman's voice as if she were in there with us in this black cave of blanketed mist. "He comes," she said. "He comes. Be still."

For this there was no answer from us because neither could we move or open our lips to speak. We were engulfed, trapped in silence now. We heard only: "It is finished. He is come."

Time passed. But we did not know how much time. We waited curled like baby squirrels soon to be born.

Then, all of a sudden, the blanket darkness was thrown off us and light seared our eyes.

Sun Father was there.

"Who are these?" he asked.

His voice was beautiful to hear and terrible at the same time.

Nayenezgani was the first to speak. "Are you our father?"

Sun Father said nothing. He grabbed both boys by the back of the neck and threw them across the room where there were gleaming spikes, like icicles, made of white shell. "Use your spider woman feathers!" I said to both, and they held them out and the spikes were as if soft and yielding. We bounced harmlessly.

Sun Father was impressed. "Let it be so," he said.

But soon after, he brought forth a smoking pipe of turquoise.

"Try this, if you think you are my sons," he said.

I whispered to Tobachischin, "Remember the ointment in your ears."

He said this same to his brother and all of us put on the sphinx vomit tobacco worm ointment and straight away we could feel the smoke of the Sun Father pass through without harm.

"Show that you like this great gift," Sun Father said, "and I will give you another." We all puffed prodigiously, and enormous clouds of smoke rose up all around us and Sun Father said, "it is good." Then he produced a jet pipe in which was even stronger tobacco, and we smoked that but it had no effect except that we sweated a lot.

"Thanks, my father, for the excellent smoke," Nayenezgani said, and handed the jet pipe back to Sun Father.

"Let it be so," he said. But I could see he was surprised the boys were so strong.

After this moon carrier came and dug a pit and we three were told to get into it. The pit was covered with a blanket of white shell, turquoise, abalone and darkness.

Sun Father poured a jar of water on the hot flints inside the pit. We were told then to get in and be warm as this sweathouse was a sacred one used by Sun Father.

We did as we were told.

At first the heat crept up on us.

The flints that held the heat of the coals underneath grew warmer and warmer.

The darkness curtain that kept all light out of the sweathouse was beginning to be charred from the heat. But yet our skin swam with sweat, we didn't feel it. Both boys had a protective necklace of white shell.

Sun Father asked, "Are you burning up in there?"

Nayenezgani answered, "Not yet."

Sun Father looked in a little later, said: "Burning?"

"Not so much," Tobachischin said, "it's warm the way we like it."

Tobachischin said, "Barely warm."

More heat came from the flints.

Soon they were throbbing red.

But the white shell kept the flint heat from scorching us.

Finally, Sun Father asked a fourth time and the boys told him they were good, the sweathouse was just like the one at home on earth.

It was then that Sun Father said, "May it be that you are indeed my children. Children of the sun. Able to defeat my guardians with kind words, able to bounce freely from my wall spikes, capable of smoking the jet and the turquoise pipe filled with sun tobacco, and now at the end of the trial of flesh, strong enough to withstand the sun's own sweathouse. Let it be so."

I wondered if I, too, having passed the same test as the Hero Twins, was a kangaroo rat of consequence, a rodent hero. Or was I just a tiny human hidden in a robe of fur?

Chapter Forty-Three

Then Sun Father took the boys to the back of the house of the sun. The back faced north where it was dark as night; this was because it was night there.

Sun Father took them to the corral where he kept five horses. Four were for the different times of day on earth. But one was a night horse, only ridden at night when the moon was up and the stars were bright.

Nayenezgani liked the horse whose name was Nightway.

Tobachischin stepped back from the corral, for this horse was bigger than any of the ones on earth, broader of shoulder and chest. When he stomped the ground shook. And the breath from his nostrils was hotter than the sweathouse.

"Who is the little man in fur you have on your shoulder?" Sun Father asked.

Tobachischin answered. "He is one of our guardians. He is wise to the ways of the world, this one and the ones below."

Sun Father came near to me, and I couldn't see anything but a blinding corona of light.

"The small," he said, "are sometimes greater than the large."

"I have witnessed him hand trembling," Tobachischin said. "He has saved us more than once."

"Then I give him my blessing."

I shivered all over, hearing that.

Then Sun Father placed an evening blanket with woven moons and stars on it, and this he put on Nightway. He bridled him with reins of jet. He led him out of the corral of darkness and we were told to ride him down to earth.

"Remember," he said, "this is no ordinary animal. Watch out when he throws his head, sparks, too, may come from his flint hooves. Avoid the scorpion in the sky. Be careful of the blood-speckled star bear, as he will try to claw you as you ride by him. Once you get to the rainbow bridge you will be safe, but you already know that because that is how you came here. Be ever cautious of Nightway. I fear to give you a gift of death. But should you boys master him, you will be able to ride him to battle on earth."

"To battle?" Nayenezgani said.

Sun Father said, "You must kill the monsters that have eaten up all the game down there. When you have done so, I will release more game animals so that The People will have food to eat again. There will come a mighty river of animals. Deer, buffalo, antelope, and sheep. So see to it that you make it to earth. You are hero twins, and with your small guardian, you will prosper and bring harmony."

And so we bid him goodbye and traveled across the night sky.

It was, at first, a velvet road of darkness, star-flecked and moon-swathed.

Nayenezgani said boastfully, "I thought this was going to be hard. It is easy."

No sooner had he said this than Nightway, who seemed to have heard him, threw his head to the side. Nayenezgani was riding high on the great horse's spine, with his legs twined around Nightway's neck. But Tobachischin and I were more toward the rear. We lost our balance with that head-swing, and fell to the side, clinging to mane and tail. Meanwhile Nightway felt his freedom and surged downward.

We clung, I, to a single strand of horse hair; Tobachischin, to a handful. Stars sang past us, falling as we fell.

Meanwhile Nayenezgani grabbed at the flapping, flinging, jetted reins of which he had lost control.

The reins whistled at our ears. The hooves pounded the star grasses.

Below us now we saw the rainbow road, that was horse-shaped. The dawn was spreading below; the whole of earth was lighting up.

But still we dropped downwards, out of control.

Nightway had his teeth sunk into the moon-bit of the bridle.

Nayenezgani made one last try to capture the loose and flying reins.

His reach was wide, long, and strong.

He got it, hauled back on it, as hard as he could. I saw that his grip was not mortal. He was a god. The boy was no longer a boy. But I was still a mouse clinging to a silver-black thread of horsehair. I glanced over my shoulder at Tobachischin. He too had mastered it—he was back on the rump of Nightway, his left hand thrown back for me to grasp. But I couldn't reach it. My hand being too small and my body too little. I clung as before. I was no god. I was a mortal mouse. But I saw that if I trembled I could go directly into the body of Nightway, and this I did. Why hadn't I thought of this before?

Suddenly I was horse. Muscled and flanked. Hooved in power.

I slammed madly through the peach-stained dawn.

Foam flew out of my nostrils.

My sides streamed with rivers of white.

I hammered down. Hurtling to earth like a comet destined to crash and burn.

Down, down, down.

I braked against clouds and they tore into pieces as I blew through them.

We landed in a fountain of fine powdered dry spray.

Diamonds of mica dust raised up from the parched desert ground.

We had come to the end of the ride.

My chest heaved. My ribs ached. My head burned.

But we had made it to earth.

And I somehow knew that someone, seeing our sudden landing, would shout, possibly to no one but himself, "Now there is a fallen star!"

Chapter Forty-Four

So I carried the Hero Twins on my back and we rode into the dawn seeking monsters.

Nayenezgani wore the armored flints of horned toad and so did Tobachischin. They carried quivers of arrows, or I should say I carried them, for I did, and each arrow was made from a bolt of lightning. All these were bundled and gifted to us by Sun Father who saw that we were well fed and fully armed.

Looking into my eye, he had seen something. I don't know exactly what it was but I believe he saw into me and knew that I was an odd, clever little rat who would turn into a proud war horse.

Armed and ready, we traveled through the canyons hoping to cleanse the land of stone giants, cactus beasts, batwind devil birds, and the others including Yeitso, the gray giant, made of flesh and fur.

So we danced off into the morning to do our work, which was to kill. We went into the killing sands to destroy that which had been made by women in the time of transgression. Some know the story; most don't. But the truth is, when the men separated from the women in the time of beginnings, the women said, collectively, "We don't need you anymore. We have found other things."

By which they meant they could please themselves in other ways and there was no need of having men do it for them. But that, so the words are told, came to be their undoing. They gave birth to monsters. All of that happened long, long ago. But yet the past informs the future, and the women lived to regret their ways on the opposite side of the river from the men who longed for them to come back and be women again.

Not until the monsters are dead and gone, was how Sun Father said it. He had told us the story and we listened by the corral before we left on Nightway, I mean, of course, me. The me that is now, so to say. But I know, beyond all measure of things known, that I will change again—and soon. My plan was to make it very soon because being a horse was not like being a kangaroo rat.

My body was a proud and powerful thing. But my mind, though filled with a certain kind of wisdom, historical sight, I would call it, was slow compared to my mouse self which was quick and eager to make things happen around me.

My horse self was strong, admirable in most ways, but a horse's mind is with the wind of change and always eager to move. Whereas the mouse skitters and dances and changes second-by-second. But can also wait. Can sit and wait for change to come. The horse is the carrier of destiny. The mouse is the warrior of little things. The mouse has no interest in history; only the moment. And in the moment, he is the fastest thinker, the quickest mover.

But now I was horse and had no choice but to bear the burden. If I could get the boys through this time of upheaval, then I could give it all up and go back to whence I came. I know it sounds strange to speak like this, but you remember, it is the horse that speaks, not the mouse or even the man that came before the mouse. It is all very confusing, I grant you.

Yet here we were on the battle plain. Weaving in and out of the canyons looking for the monsters that the world must be ridded of. This was our task and I knew we might die trying to accomplish it. But if history were in our favor, and I knew this could be so because I was a history horse, a horse like no other.

I danced on, marching as to war.

And we found it.

Or it found us.

Nayenezgani sang the songs of sorcery.

Tobachischin didn't sing.

I snorted, myself.

And so it was that the big-winged, batwind beast of the air came at us and Nayenezgani reached into the quiver of endless arrows and killed him, and all others that came within sight. The lightning, zigzag arrows, returned after passing through bat flesh.

It rained blood. Bat after giant bat died a devilish death.

And fell at our feet.

Gerald Hausman

The blazing arrows returned and were quivered. Lightning does that. It comes only to return. One arrow struck four directions at the same time, and having found many marks, returned, was quivered.

And when the giant bats were no more, the brothers urged me on.

Nayenezgani killed stone giants and they groaned and avalanched and made mountains when they crashed to ground. Their blood made rivers and when it stopped flowing it turned the desert sand to purple.

It was Tobachischin though who slew the cactus creatures, who stood forth like men, needled and secure in their place. He had a zigzag lance given to him by Sun Father and when the cactus monsters began to march he poked them in the heart, spilled their yellowish blood and that made the sand golden. Their pink blood popped out and became those fruits that are good to eat. But, one by one, they fell to arrow or lance and then shriveled like mushrooms that never see the force of the sun.

A long day's work was done by day's end.

There was but one monster left, and that one was Yeitso.

It was I who had word with him, and in fact slew him with language.

The boys were resting and eating roasted meat by a fire they'd built, the sun was setting, and along came Yeitso. We heard him coming from a long way away. And there he was suddenly looming, the sun sinking over his right shoulder and the moon perched like a parrot's head on his left.

I walked forward to face him.

He had his club that swings two ways.

That clever club I had seen before. In fact, if you will remember, I trembled into gila monster—this was when I was yet a man—and used Yeitso's two-hearted, double-swinging axe on him.

I said to him now, "Before I was horse as you see me now and before that when I was mouse and then kangaroo rat and before that when I was owl and dove and so on and so forth, I was once, and will be again, a man. It was as a man that I slipped into the red and black skin of gila monster, who, as you should recall, killed you, Yeitso. But it seems you live again, or perhaps it is just your likeness."

"That was my brother," he said, and laughed. "I will kill you now."

162

Then he struck at me with his two-swinging sharp-edged axe.

I did some beautiful foot, or rather, hoof work then.

This naturally confused him, as I went round and round the giant until he was so dizzy he couldn't stand and thus fell.

In this weakened posture, I took him by storm.

My hooves attacked his jaw and broke it into pieces, and I saw then the broken bits of shell that were his protection that he kept moist in his mouth. They fell on the desert floor and the wind from my flailing hooves took them away.

He said to me, "Is this how it ends, horse?"

And I said, "For now."

My hooves of jet came down sudden and cracked Yeitso's skull in half and white datura moths came fluttering out of the fragmented bone head of the dying gray giant. I then danced on his bones until there was nothing left of him but reddish sand, and so it remains in that place to this day.

When I got back to the boys, they were smoking jimson weed and making a lot of noise. Even the normally quiet Tobachischin was noisy, and a little crazy. Both of them singing and dancing now that their spirit task was complete.

They had forgotten that I was there. Had forgotten that I had gotten them here, down to earth from the distant house of the sun, they had forgotten all of it in this moment of dancing and singing and forgetting.

And that is the way the world is.

The hoop of life is always rolling.

Chapter Forty-Five

My horse life was over and done.

I could feel it in my horse bones. Willing my head to go forward, it nevertheless pulled back. My hooves turned toward the sun. My entire being was being willed to the west, to the sky, to the sun. I had no choice but to submit to the power greater than my own. To the power of the Sun Father.

At the same time, I felt my own power shrinking, lessening.

What was I, if not what I shaped myself into?

At this point, I let go. Gave up.

Immediately, I saw another kangaroo rat. It was chewing a cactus fruit on a stone. I could be that rat, I said to myself.

My hooves rose and I reared up.

I whinnied for my release from the great muscled horse I was, had been, and was now leaving in physical form.

Into the chew-face kangaroo rat, I went and watched from the sanctity of a flat stone in the desert as Nightway took leave of the earth and pounded skyward. The sky darkened. Stars burned. The moon turned. The horse as I saw it from below … from the large round wondering eyes of a rat … became smaller and smaller in the sea of night. For a moment, the horse's mane sparkled with stars, then … there was nothing there.

I was rat, eating as I hadn't done in days, feasting on cactus fruit. The juice dripped down my furry chin.

Now what? I asked myself.

But I had no answer other than to eat and keep eating.

I stuffed myself with mesquite seeds.

With juniper berries.

With desert roots and herbs.

Then I drank dew.

Now what? I asked again. Feeling full, stuffed, and content, I wandered off the stone seat, and found myself on the track of other mice.

The darkness hid me from some predators. But not all. I saw with my night eyes the flash of fox and coyote. The dark wing swipe of owl. Even the foot pads of wolf were out on such a starry night.

I came to a place then that seemed familiar. I smelled its ancient earth odor. There was a death smell there, but a life smell as well. Stones give off a fragrance in the moonlight. I sniffed, and remembered. This was the hole where I came down from above, long ago it seemed to me now. A lifetime ago.

I followed the familiarity.

It led me to the tunnel down which I had come in yet another form of mouse. I liked better being a kangaroo rat, but there was something wrong. I felt tired. Very tired and perhaps even old. I shook it off and went up the curving tunnel that led ever upward.

Was this going to the fifth world?

The four worlds below had been cleansed of monsters. I remembered that. Even as I crawled, mousewards up, I faintly recalled my gone life as a night-horse of the Sun Father. The boys? Oh, yeah. The boys who were the sun's sons. Where had I left them?

I remembered. But you must remember—a rat's intelligence is rather fine but a rat's memory is less than fine. He remembers only what he needs to remember, and the memory of the boys, the Hero Twins, was fading. Was their memory of the mouse who protected them and the horse that guided them also fading?

On I crawled and pulled. I drew myself along the spiral walls of the tunnel which at times was narrow and at other times wide, but always it slanted upward.

As I went with it, I had sudden bursts of memory.

There was my mouse woman, Lara, no, Laura.

What was I thinking?

Laura, my earth wife, human wife, two-legged wife. She was no mouse woman. What was I thinking?

I kept climbing.

Little tendril roots tickled my whiskers. Was I gaining on the tunnel? Was I getting closer to higher ground where things grew out of the earth. The sandy soil had turned now to stone through which the roots cracked rock and hung helplessly in the shadows. I could see well enough in darkness. But then … light shot through the tunnel.

I could see it was coming to an end.

The fifth world?

Sun Father had spoken of it.

I pushed forward, and up, and all at once, I was out of the tunnel.

The air was chill. I looked around me, sniffing.

I knew where I was … the deadhouse of … who was it?

A man called Appleplum.

My mind was back, working.

Tremble?

I needed to tremble out of this place.

It stank of human death.

Where could I go?

There were no creatures here to tremble into.

Hadn't I once been a dove? Next an owl.

And there was a blue face man at the window.

I glanced in that direction. Nothing. It was night above as it was in the fourth world below. What was I to do? Run in wet grass as a kangaroo rat and maybe get taken by yet other predators. Suddenly I missed my human, two-leggedness. And my Laura. I wanted badly to be a man again.

And then I saw my opposition. The thing that would prevent me from changing into humanness.

It was, believe me or not, Appleplum himself.

Or itself …

He stood in the inky shadows of the deadhouse, eating something.

A rat, it looked like. A me.

He looked down, suddenly.

And saw me standing, four-footed and small, undecided, at his feet.

"Ah," he said, "you are returned. I have been waiting for you, my little shapeshifting friend. I have been waiting. To eat you. I eat all kinds of little things—and big things, too."

"What are you?" I squeaked.

He heard me and grinned.

"You and those silly boys. You thought you killed all of the monsters down below in the fourth. Ah, but you missed one last cactus creature—me!"

"I saw you bleed and die with the others," I said.

"So you say. We of the cactus blood do not die so easily, little friend. Or should I even call you that? Little pestilence, with which I will extinguish all life on this ridiculous planet. I am done with it. Done with hiding and secretly dining on human beings. With the new and powerful Hanta mouse, I will finally get rid of all pestilences that walk, crawl, and slither."

"New and powerful? What are you talking about?"

Appleplum gave me a crooked smile, revealing needle teeth.

"I've infected the lot of little slinking vermin, of which you have unfortunately shapeshifted into, and the planet's on its way to being undone by one of its own kind, the most common kind there is, the rat. Who knew? Everybody knew, or knows, rats have always carried the plague. All I had to do was bring it back, and that I have done. To perfection, I would say. And now you, little pokeface, let's join your infected cousins, shall we?"

Faster than I could think, he dropped down and grabbed me. His greenish spiky hands grew larger and larger until they encompassed the world. Captured, I had no defense, especially since I noticed that the body I'd trembled into was old, maybe ancient. My teeth were old, too. As were my bones, which accounted for why it was so hard for me to climb out of the tunnel. And that is where Appleplum threw me now. Back into the tunnel.

"Bye, ratty," he said.

I tumbled through space.

Back down to the bottom of the tunnel.

Chapter Forty-Six

Falling is one thing, falling forever, is another.

I fell forever. So it seemed.

As I fell I saw the hateful face of Appleplum, child-raper, wounder of worlds, monster.

I fell and all that I had crawled passed before my eyes.

And landed …

Finally.

In the arms of Tobachischin.

I couldn't have been more surprised than he was.

But he said, "I came to give you this, and this."

And he placed a war feather in my paws.

After that, he put more of tobacco worm's vomit in my ear. "Remember," he said, "this must go from ear to mouth, but only when the smoke is thickest."

He looked at me deeply. "There will be smoke," he said. "Applecactus anus," as we call him has amassed an army of living monsters from our lower world, the fourth. You are of the fifth world. Go above and fight him. We will send you help, if you should require it. Meanwhile you have the tobacco worm's medicine and here is more. This from my brother. It is called sah-oh-yalth, old age killing medicine."

"Is that what Nuthatch gave us that time?"

"No, it comes from the place in the earth where the four points meet. One point gray, one point darker gray, one point darker than that, and the last point, white. It is what happens when we age from gray to white. One sprinkle of sah-oh-yalth and your enemy becomes old before your eyes. Then, ancient. Then, death. And dust."

He looked at me for a time to see if I under stood everything he was saying. Then he gave me the small medicine bag.

"Remember," he said at last, "you have great power now. Here is more."

He placed in my hand another potion of power; Nuthatch dust. "This is to cast into the many eyes of Applecactus anus. He sees through those buds that are all about his green skin. Cast the powder there and you will blind him, but only for a little while. You must cut him to size after you cast the Nuthatch dust. He will throw smoke at you and you will throw the vomit of the tobacco worm at him. Keep the feather over your heart and it will protect as well. He cannot kill you without first cutting out your heart. That is why I say to place the feather right here on your upper chest."

"What will hold it there?" I asked.

"It will stay of its own right. Now tell me what you will do in the order that you will do it."

I replied, "First I will seek to blind him."

"You will not seek. You will blind."

"Yes," I added, "I will blind. Then I will cast the old age medicine. The vomit of the tobacco worm I will hide in my ear until ..."

"No, little one. You will have it in your mouth before you enter into battle. Only then will you be protected from the evil smoke of the enemy. Know that there will be smoke. That is for certain. Also remember, you have to kill him. He is the last of the monsters and he must die."

"Is there anything else?" I asked.

"There is one thing more. Know that you will have help. I cannot go up above into the fifth, but there are those who can, and I hope, will. Now I must go and you must return to that place above where he awaits you. This is our destiny. You shall fulfill the prophecy or die trying to do so."

He disappeared into the darkness of the tunnel, a shadow among shards of shadows.

When he was gone I glanced at the floor of the cave and saw but one footprint.

I turned and moved upward into the tunnel that spiraled into the fifth world.

This time the long climb hurt my body. I scraped my fur against rock-stones, and I bled. I knew that I was old. But kangaroo rats do not show their age. I knew I must hide my aches and pains, and I dragged myself upward the way I had come only a short while before. As I climbed, I rehearsed what I must do at the top of the tunnel. Each of the medicines had their proper order.

The feather was there over my heart. I could feel the strength of it. The feather's power came in waves of warm vibration, making me feel stronger than I was.

Thus I climbed.

And the tunnel, in time, began to brighten into the darkest light of day.

When he saw me ascending, I started shaking.

His ugliness awaited me. The squarish head, the yellow needle teeth, the arms covered with spores of pink bud bleeding ooze of cactus sap. That he was human, too, was hard to believe. He had hands, didn't he? Hands to grasp and choke the life out of me.

My heart beat faster but I could feel the feathered down against my throbbing chest. The heat in my ear warmed the left side of my head. And the soft Nuthatch bag tied to my right wrist. Tied to my left wrist was the sah-oh-alth killing potion.

Would I be quick enough to use my weapons?

Then I remembered …

Tobachischin had said I must cut the monster up.

But I had no knife.

Nowhere to get one now.

I saw his face looming at the opening.

Chapter Forty-Seven

Circling the creased and ridged greenface of the monster was the enemy smoke Tobachischin had warned me of—the same smoke used by Sun Father. One breath of this could be the end. I hung suspended on a juniper root. I used my paw to scrape some of the hardened oil vomit of the tobacco worm. My paws were clumsy to this purpose and I accidentally dropped a little cake of the life-saving substance. The rest I got into my mouth and once again tasted the awful bitterness that made me want to throw up, but I gritted my mouse teeth and held it back.

"Come to papa, little fool," the monster said, his head like a pocked green moon very near my own.

What was it, Tobachischin called him? Apple-anus. No, that wasn't it. Appleplumcactusanus? I laughed in spite of myself. It helped. The fear backed off a little.

I was but one small remove from him now.

My last thrust drew me over the tunnel's lip and I found myself in the deadhouse on my back staring into the thousand red blood, bud eyes of the monster who raped daughters and who spread disease and death and was about to kill me.

The smoke came first. Huge billows of it. Dark deadsmoke thick as cloth. One breath would fell a giant. But I had eaten enough of tobacco worm's antidote to keep me alive. The smoke writhed and held me prisoner for a moment and then seeing it could not kill me began to lower itself, snake-like, and slide across the deadhouse floor.

I felt the needles of his hands then. They were at my throat.

His red eyes bugged out. "What is this, fool?"

He grabbed at my paws, seized them.

I felt the throbbing of my heart against the feather protector.

He snatched the medicine bag of Nuthatch powder.

At the same time, I saw behind him, as blue as the monster was green, a familiar old face. The blue face man. Was he a protector too?

"Don't forget me," the blue face man said.

He was close and I recognized him at last. He was someone I had once known. Angel Gomez.

"I thought you died," I said.

"I did," he said, with that same old laugh. "But that doesn't mean I can't help an old friend." And so saying, he leaped at Appleplum's throat.

The two of them rolled in the dust of the deadhouse, and I slipped free.

As they struggled, I caught sight of Nuthatch's medicine bag which had fallen from the cactus spikes of Appleplum's clawed hands.

I got it, opened it, poured the blinding filaments into buds of Appleplum's eyes, which bled sap yellow blood and shriveled shut. At least, then, two of his eyes couldn't see. But he had many others. I was out of powder.

For a time I did nothing but watch. What could I do?

Gomez had him by the neck and he had Gomez by the neck.

It was then I saw Appleplum's reinforcements.

They came in rows and tiers. More cacti monsters than I could count.

It was like a Roman legion of them, one stacked behind the other and as many as there were particles of dust in the deadhouse.

What could anyone do against such odds?

More particularly, what could an aged kangaroo rat and a dead man do against such strength of force?

The monsters marched on. I felt the myriad needles of their feet go into my poor rat fur and flesh. It was then I remembered the sah-oh-yalth bag tied to my right wrist. As I was being trampled and felt my life crushed between the green glob feet of the multitude of monsters, I unloosed the four points going down, one gray, darker gray, even darker, and then the white. Like a great blanket these spread out as spider woman had once told us they would and as Tobachischin promised. I knew that this final dust would end my life. But I was not so happy with this ending-life of a kangaroo rat anyway. And what could this medicine do against Angel. His name itself said everything. Bless him, and I did as he rolled with the blind-eyed, green beast of ages. I saw only the fragmental faces as they spun—the green face, the blue, the green, the ...

As for the multitude armed forces, they'd now gone from green to gray. Their arms dripped like yellowy candlewax. Death honey leaked from their rubber lips, they sank to their knees and began to grow smaller and smaller until there was nothing there but bright, moon-forged, pointed, darning needles, piles and piles of them.

And still Angel and Appleplum rolled.

And kept rolling right out of the deadhouse.

Down the hill over the prairie dog town, across the highway where traffic came to a halt. I thought of the dazed drivers seeing such a show of spinning supernaturals rolling all the way to Albuquerque.

There was that same dove in the rafters.

The one I'd ridden in once before.

I trembled out of the broken-body kangaroo rat, and flew into the living ringneck express, which brought me home.

Chapter Forty-Eight

My father used to say, "Time is of the essence."

He also used to say, whenever he saw me in the bathroom getting ready for school, "Didn't I see you here yesterday?"

Towards the end of his life, he said, "Time is a little hole in the ground into which things disappear."

And, at the very end, when he was dying, he said, "I feel I am on a mountain road in a sports car. I am going too fast and the car has no brakes. I see a cliff up ahead which drops down the sea. I know I'm going off the edge but I still don't know when ... seconds can last lifetimes."

I was thinking about my dad and the things he said to me when I came into our apartment and Laura said, "Oh, there you are!"

"I've been away," I said.

"Not more than a few minutes," she said.

She was making the bed.

I asked numbly, "Are you making the bed?"

"Anybody can," she said.

"How?" I asked.

"You have to crawl in and out, you know. Between the wall and the bed."

"We ought to move the bed so it's not so tight in there when you're making it." I laughed. "Sounds like sex ..."

"Everything sounds like sex," she said.

The way she was standing against the wall, her hips slightly canted, as she bent gently to the sheets and blankets, straightening them out, I saw something I remembered and could never forget. One year when we were very poor and I was trying to write and make money and was having a hard time of it, she decided to help out by hiring herself out as a nude model.

It would drive me crazy thinking about her standing naked in front of strangers at an art class or a photo shoot.

So, one day, I asked her if she would pose for me.

"What will you be doing?" she asked.

"Watching."

"Why?"

"Because you are so lovely to look at."

She did that for me then, and she was so beautiful, and just for me, that I never felt envious again of those absent and unknown strangers who saw her as naked as the day she was born.

***

In the time I'd been gone I'd lived several lifetimes.

Or so it seemed.

There is a great urgency, a restlessness you feel after the change, the tremble. You don't know exactly where you fit, how you feel, exactly.

You wander around picking up books, looking at them but not reading. You stare at the snowy mountains wondering how much runoff will be flowing in the river and whether there will be ravens. And always, if you are me, you get pulled to one side, as if there was a giant magnet near you that would slowly and inexorably bring you to it.

The magnet, in my case, was the deadhouse.

I'd forbidden myself to go into it again.

Was it all a dream?

I went down there, slipped between the break in the fence, and looked at it. A fallen down adobe house from another century. That was all. There was a light snow, but no tracks. A wispy bit of smoke circled above the half-smashed chimney. I went to the deadhouse, stepped inside. A man was tending the fire. A sweet smoke filled the shadow space of the long rectangular room.

He turned, glanced over his shoulder. "So, it's you," he said.

"Gomez?"

"Yeah, it's me."

I came closer. "You look pretty beat up," I said.

"Thanks," he said. "I feel good though. Got rid of that bastard, once and for all, I hope. We tumbled all the way down to La Bajada hill where I finally got the better of him. Pushed the green cocksucker into a semi, crushed his head into a green gel, but you know, that damn toothy grin of his was still there pressed flat to the road after the truck had eight-wheeled him. It was kind of like he was laughing at me out of the mess that used to be his head. His body was flat as a piece of green tarpaper. I shoveled up the lot of it with a hubcap, what was left of the monster fucker, and burned him to shit. Green shit."

He shook his head. "Maybe he'll come back. Maybe he won't."

"You came back."

He looked at me for a while, then shook his head again.

"Got nothing better to do."

I asked him, "Do others come back, like you, I mean. You know, on a mission."

He spat, and nothing came out of his mouth.

"I got no mission," he said.

"Must be lonely."

"Not really. And, hell yes. It depends."

"Are you lonely now?"

"Not talking to you. But after you go, I might be lonely again. Not everyone can see me or hear me. Sometimes they can do one but not the other. It's all messed up until you get used to it. I saw Buffalo Bill the other day, you know, William F. Fucking Cody, and he still doesn't know whether to work those rodeo shows or just sit around and ride his horse. Speaking of that horse, he seems to have a better handle on the afterlife than old Bill."

Gomez took a crumpled piece of paper out of his pocket. The handwriting was illegible and smudged, but he could read it just the same:

" 'On a good day,' the horse told me, "I could take Bill eighty miles uphill and down dale between nightfall and sunup. Most times I'm good for fifty miles a day and there's not an arroyo, a niche, or a notch I haven't been. Hell, I've gone thousands of miles with old Bill, and his backside was sore but I kept on going, that's how it is when you're a horse. There's not a hill or a sawdust circle I haven't dropped a poop on, and that's all I have to say about this!'"

"Buffalo Bill's horse told you this?"

Gomez nodded. "I don't get lonely talking to horses that have that kind of get-up-go, it's people that tire me out. They don't get it. Whether you're dead or alive, you live. That's all there is to it. And that's what Bill's horse was telling me. He's as alive as he ever was. Think of it, most living people worry all the time about dying. Then, once they're dead, they worry about being alive."

I looked into the fire.

When I looked back at Gomez he wasn't there.

Chapter Forty-Nine

I suppose I was in recovery from the events I have described. As usual, it was Jay who came to my rescue by explaining the nature of stars. I already knew how they contained the essential elements of the Navajo laws of existence. But I still wondered about the metaphysical components, or mechanics of good stars, bad stars and the like.

I was telling Jay, while we ate fry bread made by his wife Ethel, "I still don't understand how there could be bad stars in the heavens. Especially if the whole Navajo cosmology is based on harmony."

"Well," he said, "it all started around the time of the great flood. Just after the flood, my father said."

He took a little sip of the chamomile tea I had made for him. I had a cup of piñon roast dark blend coffee, as did Laura. Ethel wasn't drinking anything. She was patting dough and frying it. The sound of that frying made George think of the rainforest. Whenever there was frying, he started singing.

"So," Jay went on, smiling at George, "First man and first woman knew that the people wanted more light so they could see the new world that was made for them after the flood waters. The people were told to put offerings on the wings of bat. The people did this and the offerings turned into stars ..."

I had never heard that one before and I told him so and he nodded. We both kept eating the fry bread Ethel made. Jay continued, "But, you know, since the stars did not have life in them yet, the pollen boys were asked to sing life into them. They began to do this but coyote came along. He stole the boys' voices. So the stars didn't flicker the way they were supposed to. After that the people gave coyote offerings. He accepted them. Then he sang to the different directions—east, south, west, and north. Then light was breathed into the stars and they began to shine."

Jay paused and looked out the window. "Did you always have those magpies?" he asked.

"That's a funny story," I told him. "One morning the mother magpie came into the house through the open back window. She hopped up onto our bed and woke us up. She actually pecked me softly on the lips."

Jay smiled. "They do that sometimes. Rarely."

I said, "It turned out she wanted me to put her nestling back up in the nest. I got a ladder and did that, and these magpies have been our friends ever since."

Jay smiled some more and we both ate more fry bread. Then Ethel said, "I'm tired of making fry bread, think I'll sit down for a little while."

"Coyote messed with the constellations after that," Jay said. "He got them all scattered, so first man and first woman had to rearrange them and make them right."

"Coyote screws up everything," I said.

"Someone has to," Jay said. "There's creation and destruction, and creation again."

"So then what happens?" I asked.

Jay licked some honey off his first finger and said, "Coyote later said to the people, 'I'm sorry for what I did but don't be mad at me because I will be the one to call for rain and you will also need me for other things which I can explain at another time.'"

"But what about the bad stars?"

Jay thought about this for some moments. Then he nodded to himself. "I think I heard one medicine man, not my father, say that only the dark stars, the dark blue and the black ones, were evil."

"—And why is that? Because you can't see them clearly?"

"Often you can't see them at all. They come down to earth in the form of persons, and sometimes they are very ill-willed and contrary, and this one medicine man said that the people who can see them do bad things."

"You mean," I suggested, "they do bad things because of the influence of those stars?"

"It can work the other way, too."

"The stars are influenced in a negative way by the people who use, or abuse them."

"Something like that." Jay looked out at the magpies. "Those birds," he said, "can go either way. You gave them good vibrations and helped them, they thank you for that by being your guardians. They tell you if something bad is going to come. They ward off interlopers. But let's say, you treated them badly, let's say you didn't return that baby to the nest, you let it die instead. That would bring out the bad in the magpie and you'd be plagued."

"You know the expression, thank your lucky stars?"

Jay nodded. "I've heard of it."

"The Elizabethans believed everything harmonious came from the stars. For the same token, they thought that ill-starred lovers couldn't have harmony in their lives simply because the stars were against them."

Jay chuckled. "They were like Navajos," he remarked. "That's why, in the sand-paintings, the medicine man always puts a rainbow as a shield over the heads of the different stars. These are harmony stars with harmonious protectors over them."

I told him, "The lyfe so short, the craft so long to learne."

"Who said that?"

"Geoffrey Chaucer, storyteller from the middle ages."

"There's no price on the head of wisdom," Jay said.

"Or favorable stars," I added.

Chapter Fifty

In Jay's world a subject was never really closed. Some days after we had met and talked about the stars he phoned me.

"You know," he said, "there's all kinds of things going on up in the heavens we don't usually talk about. For instance, there's a lot of sex going on up there. The ones you call Orion and the Pleiades, these had sexual union and there were two daughters who were born of this. One was called Old Age Living Long and the other was Happiness Comes From It."

Jay chuckled at what he'd just said.

"There's more," he said. "These two daughters eventually had sex with the Sun Father and they gave birth to the ones we call Seven Flint Boys. These Flint Boys are fun to watch. You will notice that the seventh son tags along after the other six. He tags because that is his habit."

"Is this like Coyote, the mischief maker?"

Jay chuckled again. "It's kind of funny. It's not always the ones who are in the lead who are wise. Often it's the goofs, the screw ups, who help straighten things out on earth and up above. You know, like Coyote, who messes things up and then tends to fix them up later on. Some of his corrections finally become moral laws. The same is true of the Star People."

I asked him, "What if a Star Person goes crazy and becomes, well, a sex-craved maniac. I know it sounds a bit comic-book to put it that way, but I am thinking of that guy Appleplum."

Jay said, with a kind of abrupt seriousness in his voice, "You don't think you've seen the last of him, do you?"

"I didn't know what to make of his ending on earth, if that's what it was. I mean ..."

"—If you want to see him and talk to him, why don't you build a big fire and let the sparks go up into the sky. The smoke from your fire is like Black God. He can summon the Seventh Son who will keep an eye on Appleplum ... and you, too, my friend." He laughed.

I let this sink in for a moment or two. There were always long pauses in phone conversations with Jay. Sometimes so long I imagined we'd lost our connection.

He continued after about a full minute of silence, which on the telephone, feels like a full day.

"Black God has the Milky Way on his shoulders like a serape. His permanent home is between the white star in the east, the blue star in the south, the yellow star in the west, and the pink star in the north."

"I have no idea how I'm going to use any of this knowledge, Jay."

Jay laughed again. "One of these days all the supernaturals will get together on earth, the sex-starved and the sexist and the sexless. When that big to-do takes place, all the Star People will take control of the earth. That is the prophecy anyway."

"Is that beginning to happen now?"

He yawned. "Excuse me," he said, "I need to tell you something. I can still start a fire with one match. That's what my grandchildren always say. They kid around and call me One Match."

I sensed we were done talking about the metaphysics of the starry dynamo. At the same time, I wondered if I was One Match, Two Matches or Five Matches. When I was a Boy Scout I got a merit badge for lighting a fire with flint. In those days I might have called myself One Flint. Now I wondered if I could summon Black God with five long-stemmed matches. I decided not to share this with Jay.

Chapter Fifty-One

Long ago Winnebago medicine men taught the rite of reintegration after death. A dance was done to show that a man could heal himself if he remembered the blessing of the bear.

As a hand trembler I was struck by the reference to "finger dancing" in a very old account of the reintegration of an unconscious or unalive person:

"His fingers begin dancing as the bear dancers weave all about him. The bear dancers hold out hands, supplicate, pray, offer power. Little Priest's fingers dance, then his whole arm … he sits up, rubs earth on his wounds … he stands and dances … his power completely restored."

I knew, I positively knew, what this was about and how it felt.

Once, when I was twelve, I fell thirty feet from a maple tree I was climbing. Coming down, I was whipped and torn by dead branches. My chest was covered with blood. I had the wind knocked out of me. No one seemed to know I had fallen, was badly injured, was only semi-conscious. But I knew. I trembled with my fingers, then my whole arm, and summoned help. Lying there I seemed to pass through many lives, like the Winnebago warrior who died in battle and returned.

"Once I was at war and was killed. After my death I arose and went to my home. But my wife and children would not speak to me. I went back to the place where I had been killed, and saw my body.

"I tried to return to the place where I had lived with my family for four years, but I was unsuccessful.

"Once I was a fish. But the life of a fish is much worse than ours. They are frequently in lack of food. But they are very happy beings and have many dances.

"Once I was a little bird. When the weather was good, I liked being a bird person. But in cold weather, I suffered from lack of food. I lived in a hole in a tree. If I slept too far in, I could hardly breathe. If I slept too far out I was cold all night.

"Once I was a buffalo. I had plenty to eat and a warm coat of fur to keep me warm. But there were always hunters and I had to be on the alert.

"From my buffalo life I was permitted to go to my higher spirit home up above. There I met spirit grizzly. I learned his songs so I could sing them again back on earth. I carried a live coal in the palm of my hand and struck it with the palm of my other hand.

My hands trembled after that, and I was able to heal people."

***

So far, to my knowledge, I'd healed no one but myself, and for my own selfish purposes. But now I vowed to help others with what I could do … if I could do it.

One thing I knew. I could heal someone, if given the chance, without saying or doing anything. The art of trembling as time goes by, and when practiced often enough, becomes as nothing more than a kind intention of the mind. You put yourself into your own hands. The tremble, which had once started in childhood and was noticeable as a physical tremor, was now nothing more than a kind of intention. A lean of the mind in the direction of whatever needed attention.

I was practicing it on myself the other day at Dunkin.

That is the last place where you would expect someone to be hand trembling for the peace of the world at large.

But as I concentrated on my hands, I felt the familiar weight go into them. From my shoulders to my fingertips I felt an almost orgasmic rush, or as we used to say, a buzz. Anyway—an upliftment. But nothing moves. The hands stay where they are. The fingers are still. But underneath the skin the nerve fiber is suddenly alive with a new kind of consciousness.

The man sitting next to me looked like Geronimo.

We were there drinking our coffee in silence. Brothers of the black coffee ritual. Secret sharers of silence.

Black. No sugar. No cream.

The man turned to me and said, "Who is your favorite conductor?"

"Railroad?"

"Symphony."

I shrugged. "I don't know."

"For me," he said, "it's Ormandy, Fiedler, Leinsdorf, Ozawa."

I nodded, then said, "I stood next to Seiji Ozawa once."

The man's eyebrows raised. "Yeah, what'd he look like?"

"Small," I replied. "Intense. Nice hair."

He chuckled and asked, "You ever see Ormandy?"

My turn to laugh … "I actually lived down the street from him."

"Yeah? What'd he look like?"

"Old man in a heavy overcoat, summer and winter."

We sipped our black coffee in silence.

After a long silence, he said, "You see Ormandy, tell him I said hello."

"Ormandy's dead," I told him.

"No way," he answered. "He's still trodding the earth. Just like Geronimo."

Then he got up and left.

I noticed that his hair was blue-black and glossy, all the way down to the middle of his back.

He trembled out of Dunkin into the sun.

I trembled back into my own meditation.

It works every time," I said to myself. Some might call it magic. Others might call it qigong. My teacher did, still does. Though he says, 'Love with no exit, no end makes the hands tremble and the heart glad.'

Philip Whalen, Zen poet, told me, "There is no such thing as Zen. There is just sitting."

The empty mind is full.

The empty hands relax, wanting nothing.

Then something comes.

A spirit grizzly, a likeness of Geronimo, a lost person in need of love.

Afterword

I was in the back country again.

A hogan hunkered down into the hill so that it was barely visible. The doorway, as expected, faced east. The door had a lintel made from shapely juniper trunks and it had a blanket drawn across. The octagonal walls were stone-chinked and slabbed with mud. This was an old one, and the roof was a loom of woven juniper over which earth had been laid down long ago. Grass was growing out of it, tussocks of prairie grass.

I opened the blanket door.

A fire was flickering in the center of the red sand floor. Nearby, sitting on a dry painting of star designs, simple crosses in Navajo sandpaintings, there was an old man wearing an incongruous pair of khaki, fringed, cut-offs, shabbily made. The old man was shrunken and small. Although he was ageless, to me, I guessed his age to be somewhere well beyond ninety.

His face was blue. The medicine wings of bluebird and butterfly had dusted him.

He stared at me, blinked a couple times, turned back to the fire, the sandpainting, then, slowly, his gaze returned to me. "I knew you'd find it one day," he said with a faint smile.

"Am I too late?" I asked.

"For what?"

It struck me in that moment, hearing the distance in his voice, that he had a short time to live. Or maybe a longer time in another place, as medicine men sometimes say.

Again, he tried to smile, but failed to do so.

There was a little tear, I noticed, in his left eye.

He went on, his voice fractured with pauses. "I tried and failed."

For a while he said no more, then: "I lost. That is all."

"You lost what? And to what person or thing?"

"The star people refused me," he said with finality.

"The star people?"

"The ones you've been chasing."

"I wasn't chasing. If anything, they chased me."

"You know what I mean. That one. That Al-lan. And the other, Plum-something." He shook his head. "They have bad names."

"They are all crazy people," I said. "Most likely dead crazy. At least I know that Plum-something is. Gomez, the tribal cop, took care of that."

The old man took a deep breath. "I will have to die in order to fulfill the prophecy and join up with Kokopelli and the other stars, the good, the bad and the fairly ugly ..." He laughed and looked up at me. I was kneeling very near him now. His left eye was clouded over by cataract. His other eye was clear.

I glanced then at the sandpainting he was sitting on. It was the story of the Navajo emergence from the lower worlds. It was done well enough in colored sand: the grays, the whites, the blacks, the blues, the yellows and reds were uneven but beautiful configurations of the risen characters of the first world moving up to the second, the third, fourth and fifth worlds. This was the crucial time of beginnings. The time of ant, locust with his bow, heron with his wise beak carrying darkness, even gray giant, Yeitso, was there mis-shapen and hulking ... I noticed that his skull was cracked and the butterflies were pouring out of it.

"My work is finished," the old man said with neither regret nor worry. He just spoke facts, his voice flat and unaccented with any emotion. "The lesson I have learned in this life will go, but I will not be there to see it or know. That is why I summoned you."

"Why me?"

He did not answer, instead he said, "On the wall by the doorway there is a medicine bag made of fawnskin. Bring it to me."

I did that thing, and he said, "Look inside the bag."

I did that.

"Bring the feathers out," he directed softly.

I did that.

"Once there was a raven feather in there, but I carried that to the north where we must go after we die. It's waiting for me there. What other feathers do you have in your hand?"

"There is a heron feather, I think."

"You will take that to the east."

I nodded. "All right."

"There was a yellow feather in there, too, and I took it to the west along with a small piece of whiteshell."

"I know about that," I said.

"Good," he said.

I felt that he was finished talking, but I waited politely to see if there was anything more he wanted to say.

There was, I was sure of it. I waited.

"There is only one feather left," I said, urging him on after a long pause where the only sound was the snapping of the fire. The juniper smoke tickled my nose with its sweet, peppery desert fragrance.

"Do you know where that last feather must be delivered?"

I shook my head. "A place of blue water?"

He smiled, almost.

Then in his dry-arroyo voice, "Where the blue water is the color of turquoise, you will go. Someone there, a man who lives on a very tall rock, will take the feather, and return to you the source of all-life. I will know of this. I will feel it."

I turned the brilliant green plume to the firelight and it seemed greener and glossier in the sudden spurt of juniper light.

"What if I fail?" I asked.

He smiled for the first time. "That is not possible. For you have the most important feathers of all. Don't make me come back through the hole in rock."

He laughed.

I still hear that laugh, driving South to blue water, green feather in hand.

Coming Soon!

Star Song *series*
SUNGAZER
Book 3
by
Gerald Hausman

SUNGAZER, is the continuing adventure of journalist Jack Andrews as he uncovers more mysteries in his ongoing search for enlightenment.

In this latest inquiry into the unknown, Jack's investigative reporting takes him on an assignment from New Mexico to Jamaica where he is pursued by agents of darkness, who seek to put a stop to his investigations. Memorable characters, lunacy, magic and malevolence haunt the pages of the novel.

An SV Original Publication

For more information
visit: www.speakingvolumes.us

Coming Soon!

The Sheriff Lansing s*eries*
Legend of the Dead
Book 1
by
Micah S. Hackler

Attempting to discover the truth about a murder in the desert ridges among ancient Native American sites, Sheriff Cliff Lansing travels to the Anasazi Strip, where he encounters a second murder involving a United States senator.

For more information
visit: www.speakingvolumes.us

Now Available

"If you're hungry for a book to keep you up past bedtime—with all the lights on—this tale is for you. Based on real unsolved mysteries, *Evil Chasing Way* deals with startling animal deaths that some attribute to aliens, skinwalkers, secret government research or a force of true evil. This is New Mexico's own X File anchored in Hausman's elegant prose and finely tuned descriptions of the Southwestern landscape."

—Anne Hillerman, author of *Song of the Lion*

For more information
visit: www.speakingvolumes.us

Now Available

Stories of bravery and murder, stories of love, betrayal and suicide. Sometimes it seems that the gun is doing the talking—not for itself—but for all of us.

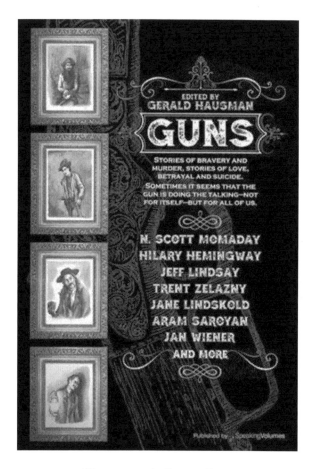

For more information
visit: www.speakingvolumes.us

Now Available

A Howard Moon Deer Mystery
Book 1

"Terrific…I couldn't put it down."
—Margaret Truman, author of *Murder at the Watergate*

For more information
visit: www.speakingvolumes.us

Now Available

A Howard Moon Deer Mystery
Book 2

"Fans of Hillerman will love this unique and quirky detective duo."
—Leslie Glass, bestselling author of *Judging Time*

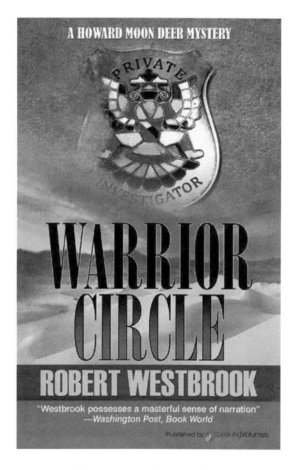

For more information
visit: www.speakingvolumes.us

Sign up for free and bargain books

Join the Speaking Volumes mailing list

Text

ILOVEBOOKS

to 22828 to get started.

Message and data rates may apply.

Printed in Great Britain
by Amazon

57507385R00123